Juliet Banks had everything she wanted in her overseas love. When a terrible accident takes him away from her, she knows her chance at love has been lost forever. That is, until she meets Hayden.

Hayden Noble is a light in the darkness that has seemed to shroud Juliet since losing the man she loved. He's gorgeous, funny, and sets her on fire with just a look. In her grief, she agonizes over whether she should give him a chance to teach her how to move on.

As their relationship deepens, a secret is revealed, one that could very well destroy all that Juliet has worked to move past. Can Juliet's heart be mended, or will her second chance at love end in more heartbreak?

The Leap
Copyright © 2019 Candace Ripley
ISBN: 978-1-4874-2239-4
Cover art by Martine Jardin

Published by eXtasy Books Inc or
Devine Destinies, an imprint of eXtasy Books Inc

Look for us online at:
www.eXtasybooks.com or www.devinedestinies.com

THE LEAP

BY

CANDACE RIPLEY

DEDICATION

For my mom, who never gave up on me even when I wanted to give up on myself.

Chapter One

I sat behind my computer tapping my pen against the desk as I stared the clock down. Two more hours and I'd be going home. Henson and Clarke Enterprises wasn't the worst place to be, but it was monotonous. Every weekday from nine to five I plugged in information and crunched numbers. I knew I was lucky I'd even gotten this job, so I tried to suck it up and power through, but today I found myself drifting. I could think of nothing other than getting home and talking to Drake.

Drake Reed was a gorgeous blond with clear green eyes and a perfect smile. I'd met him online a year ago on a message board for long-distance pen pals. We started off as friends, but it quickly grew into something more. We sent each other long letters, sent messages, video chatted, and even talked on the phone on occasion. I live in Glass Rock, North Carolina, and he lives in London, so the long-distance calling was a problem occasionally, but it was a nice treat whenever I got to hear his voice. That charming accent was more than I could handle even on my best days.

It was November now, just before Thanksgiving, and Drake was planning his first ever trip to America. In three short days he'd be coming to stay with me, and it went without saying that I was as nervous as I was excited. I'd envisioned our first meeting a million times in a million different ways, but I knew my imagination wouldn't compare to the real thing.

"Juliet, do you have that file prepared for me?"

I looked up at the sound of my name to see my manager, Carter Dunlap, standing over me.

"Oh, right, the file. Yes, I sent it to your email about ten minutes ago," I answered with a polite smile. Carter made me a little . . . uncomfortable. He was attractive physically, with chestnut-brown hair, sky-blue eyes, and a trim frame, but he tried to use those features to get away with murder. As beautiful as he was from the outside, he was twisted, dark, and ugly on the inside. He often flirted with the women in the office, bordering on harassment. I was no exception. In fact, it was well known that he came at me the hardest.

"Perfect. Thanks, beautiful." He winked and leaned in closer. "Any plans tonight?"

"Yes, I'm, uh, meeting with my boyfriend," I partially lied. I wouldn't actually be meeting with Drake yet, but I would be spending my night talking with him.

"Right, well, call me when you change your mind." He gave me a lingering smirk before straightening up and moving away.

A shiver of revulsion crawled its way through my body as I watched him prowl with unearned confidence through the office. I don't think it was an exaggeration to say every woman in the office longed for the day he was promoted to a different department or flat-out fired for being unprofessional. I didn't care which it was, as long as he left me alone.

I pulled in a breath and got back to work, trying not to think about Drake or how much I hated working for Carter. By the time five o'clock rolled around, I was shutting my computer off and scooping up my bag. Riding the elevator to the bottom floor, I punched in a text to Drake to let him know I was off work and heading home.

I was hurrying across the marble floor of the lobby when my name was called out. I turned to see my best friend,

Morgan, shuffling toward me. Morgan worked one floor up from me, so we didn't really see much of each other during the work day, but occasionally we were able to catch each other as we were leaving or we'd go out for drinks. Tonight, though, I was in a hurry to get home.

Morgan caught up with me and hugged me tightly. "Glad I caught you. What do you say to drinks down at the Harbinger tonight?"

"Can't, sorry. I have some things to do before Drake comes in," I said apologetically.

"He won't be here for three more days, Juliet. And then I won't see you again until after Thanksgiving. Please? One last hurrah before the holidays."

I chewed my lip. It was true that I wouldn't see her once Drake was in town. He was staying for a week, and I'd used all my vacation time to take that week off to spend the whole time with him.

"Okay, one last hurrah," I replied, smiling widely.

She linked her elbow through mine and steered me toward the front doors of H&C Enterprises.

The Harbinger was a three-minute walk from H&C Enterprises, so it was a popular spot for employees after the long day was over. We sank down onto stools at the bar, and a bartender came up to take our drink orders.

"I'll have a Manhattan," I told him after Morgan gave her order.

She side-eyed me and waited until the bartender turned away saying, "Skipping right to the hard stuff tonight?"

"It's been a long day." I sighed and rubbed my temples. My files had piled up before me, and I knew I had a long day ahead of me tomorrow as well.

"Carter still giving you shit?"

I shot her a *what do you think* look.

She snorted. "You have to admit the man has a great ass."

"I can admit that he's a huge ass," I grumbled. Morgan didn't have to deal with him, so she didn't understand just how bad being around him could be. She didn't have to endure his wandering gaze or his offhand comments. He hadn't actually done anything yet as far as anyone knew, so no one in the office felt comfortable taking his behavior to a senior board member.

"At least you don't have ancient Mr. McDunn hovering over you. He smells like old people and stale coffee."

I almost would have preferred it, but I didn't say anything.

Our drinks came, and I took a long sip from mine, reveling in the way the whiskey burned on the way down. Draining the cup, I held the empty glass up for a refill and peered around. A few people in work clothes were gathered around at tables, laughing and unwinding. Glancing down at my phone, I sent Drake another text letting him know I was out for a drink, but I'd be home soon if he'd still be awake. He still hadn't replied to my first message.

"Are you excited about Drake coming?" Morgan questioned with a knowing smile.

"I am, but I'm also really nervous. What if there's no spark in person like there is when we text or talk?" It was the thing that worried me the most—that he'd get here and we wouldn't click. On paper, we were perfect for one another. He was an accountant, liked chess and reading, hiked on the weekends, and I was hardly any different. I held a stable job at an investment company, also liked to read, enjoyed cooking for my friends, and though I wasn't super into outdoorsy things, I did enjoy yoga. Or used to when I had free time and energy. I was already picturing how perfect our lives would be together, how beautiful our children would be.

"Relax, it'll all be fine. He's going to take one peek at you and trip all over himself trying to make you happy. You're gorgeous and you have a great personality, things he's already aware of, so there's nothing to fear."

"You're right, I know you are." But there was that lingering doubt and fear that I wouldn't measure up.

"Then let's drink to the great sex you'll surely be having in the near future," Morgan smirked as she held her glass up.

I clinked mine to hers, then took a sip.

"If all goes well, maybe we can double date while he's here."

"Are you seeing someone?" If so, it was news to me.

"I slept with Mark from the eighteenth floor last night, and he's been begging for more." She cackled. She had what she dubbed a magic vagina.

"You're terrible" I laughed and shook my head. "I'm happy for you, though. You deserve to have someone, too."

"Oh, Mark isn't boyfriend material, but I'm willing to keep him around just for the sex."

It wasn't unusual of her. She'd had many more partners than I had. I didn't see anything wrong with it, but it just wasn't in the cards for me. I wasn't one to have a one-night stand or a fling. Mostly I was the kind of person who wanted stability and longevity.

"Well, if you're still seeing each other by the time he gets here, I'll talk to him about it," I promised. I checked my phone again, but there was nothing from Drake. I assumed he'd fallen asleep. It was a little after six, so that made it sometime past eleven for him, and I knew he had to work the next day just as I did. I felt a little disappointed that I wouldn't get to talk to him tonight. Throughout the week it was harder to stay in touch with us both working, but we tried to talk for a few minutes at least every night.

Drake had been under a lot of pressure at work, so I was

sure he was just really tired and had fallen asleep, but I couldn't get the knot of unease to untangle itself in my stomach. What if he was having second thoughts about all of this? Traveling around the world for a girl you met online was a big deal. If I were him I might be thinking twice about spending all that money to go see someone I'd never officially met, too.

Morgan threw her blonde ponytail over her shoulder and razed me to the ground with her clear, gray eyes. "You're thinking too hard, babe. Just relax a little. You need to drink up." She flagged down the bartender to order another round while I took a deep breath and tried to make myself calm down.

I pasted a smile on my face.

It was close to eleven by the time I got home from the bar. I was tipsy but not drunk, just enough to take the edge off my doubts. Shucking my heels off at the door, I traveled into the kitchen to grab a glass of water before heading to bed. It was going to be another fun-filled day of Carter tomorrow, so I needed my rest.

I preemptively took some ibuprofen for the impending headache I always got when I drank, then stripped to my underwear. After pulling clothes from my dresser, I changed into pajamas and crawled into bed. I was out within a few minutes.

An obnoxious ringing pulled me from sleep, and I palmed the bedside table for my alarm clock. It felt like I'd barely slept at all. When I smacked my alarm clock a few times, I realized that the ringing wasn't coming from the clock, but from my phone. The clock read three-fifteen. Who would be calling so late?

I snatched my phone up and groggily answered, "Hello?"

"Hello, is this Juliet Banks?" a woman with an English accent asked.

I sat up in bed. Something felt wrong — really wrong.

"Uh, yes, this is Juliet. May I ask who's calling?" I was fully awake now, no coffee needed.

"This is Tamara from a hospital here in London. There's been an accident. It seems you've been put down as Mr. Drake Reed's main emergency contact."

All the breath left me. He was hurt, and I was halfway around the world. I was already running a million options in my head as to how I'd get there to be with him while he recovered.

"What happened? Is he okay?"

The woman paused a moment then said, "I'm afraid he isn't okay He was in a car accident on his way to work this morning, and he suffered fatal wounds. I need someone to come collect his personal belongings, but if you aren't able, I can call his second emergency contact."

Fatal. She'd said fatal. "So he's . . . he's . . ." I couldn't bring myself to say the words.

"I'm so sorry." She didn't sound sorry. She sounded like she'd had to do this so many times that it didn't faze her anymore.

"No," I whispered. "No, you're wrong. He's fine."

"I'm very sorry, but I need to know who will be coming by to retrieve his things."

"I-I'm not in London right now," was all I could manage to squeak out.

"Very well, I'll call his second contact and see if they'll handle the pick-up then. I'm very sorry for your loss."

She disconnected the call, and I stared at my phone as if it were burning my palm. I hurled it across the room, listening to the distinct thump reverberate around me as it hit the wall with force.

Drake couldn't be gone. He was coming here in three

days. We were going to see each other in person finally, see if this was truly something to work for, and I felt that it was. I loved him. How could he be gone just like that?

A broken sob tore from my chest while I curled up on the bed. I cried for hours, until the sun peeked its rays in through the blinds of my bedroom window. When my alarm screamed at me to get out of bed, I rolled over and shut it off. How was I supposed to get through a work day knowing that the man I loved was no longer in this world? How was I supposed to move on from this?

I mechanically showered and dressed in more pajamas before calling work.

Carter answered. "Hello, Henson and Clarke Enterprises, Carter Dunlap speaking."

"Carter, it's me. Juliet."

"Juliet? Is everything all right?"

I sucked in a breath, but it was no use. Only a sob escaped me.

"Are you okay?"

I told him about what happened and how I needed to fast track my vacation so I could go overseas to attend the funeral. He promised me he'd work on it and call back. It might be the only decent thing the man had ever done.

I lay on my bed and stared at the ceiling, hot tears slicking the sides of my face. They wouldn't stop coming, though I was no longer hysterical. I had moved past that right on into numbness. The numbness was the only thing keeping me from panicking. I knew that would come later, so I was enjoying feeling absolutely nothing while I still could.

Hours later, Carter called back to tell me my vacation days had been moved up starting today, and I breathed a sigh of relief, thanking him. Moving from the bed, I pulled out my suitcase and threw clothes into it. I hadn't even booked a flight yet or found anywhere to stay over in

London.

I was focused on one thing and one thing only—getting my chance to say goodbye to the man I never got to meet.

CHAPTER TWO

Three months later

"I want to thank you all for coming out tonight. It's been a wonderful evening, and we want you all to know that H&C Enterprises values you all." Applause erupted from the party guests as our host for the night, none other than Carter Dunlap, finished his speech.

I politely clapped and edged toward the French doors of the ballroom for some air.

Every year in early February H&C Enterprises held a huge party to cram Christmas and New Year's into one big thing. It was always held in the Grand Bohemian Hotel in the center of town, and everyone showed up. I probably wouldn't have tonight if Morgan hadn't dragged me. I wasn't in the mood to be around a bunch of people where I'd have to dance and socialize with this false smile on my face all night.

It had been three months since Drake's death, and everyone still looked at me with pity. I hated it. I didn't want their pity or their kindness since I'd lost someone who meant everything to me.

When I stepped outside and saw that it was just as crowded as the inside, I spun on my heel and beelined for the bathroom. There were a few women taking up stalls, but it was quieter in here than it was out there. I leaned against the counter and spared a glance at myself. My unruly curly chocolate hair made me appear frazzled, and my blue-green eyes sat wide in my head. I was pale, and my face seemed gaunt from the months of grief.

Three whole months and I still wasn't over him even a little bit. When would the pain lessen into dull ache like I'd been promised it would? Tears pricked my eyes, and I blinked them away quickly. I wasn't going to fall apart, not here.

"There you are!"

I turned from the mirror as Morgan came up to me.

"They're about to announce the awards, and I have it on good authority that one of them belongs to you."

"I actually think I'm just going to go home."

Her brows drew together above her silver eyes. "What's wrong?"

Everything was wrong. It felt wrong to be enjoying a party when Drake was six feet under, unable to enjoy drinks and dancing and joviality.

"It's just a little much, I guess. I don't think I'm ready to really be out at big parties like this just yet."

She pursed her lips with sympathy and nodded. "I'll let them know you felt sick and needed to go home. I'll pick you up for brunch tomorrow at ten."

I silently thanked her before we slipped out of the bathroom, and I made my way to the coat closet.

I ambled down the sidewalk past the hotel to a small bar that boasted cheap drinks. Though I wasn't in the mood for a party, I wasn't quite ready to be home alone yet either. When I was home, the grief seemed to consume me wholly.

It was only the second week into February, so it was still freezing cold out, but the bar was warm and inviting. I sat on a stool and waited for the bartender to notice me. She smiled and headed over.

"You look mighty pretty to be in a place like this," she said with her hands on her hips.

"Yeah, I left the party next door. All they have is champagne."

She laughed and asked what I wanted.

"A Manhattan, please."

With my drink in front of me, I stared into the glass, willing it to give me the answers I needed. I didn't want to feel so heartbroken all the time. I wanted to move on with my life. At twenty-five I was far from old, but I felt well beyond my years with all the pain I was in.

Someone settled into the seat next to me, but I didn't look up until they spoke. "Rough night?" An English accent. Just like Drake.

Would I never escape him?

"Something like that," I muttered, turning my head.

He was basically Drake's polar opposite. He had dark hair that curled over his ears, and eyes so brown they were almost black. He was smiling, showing off a pair of dimples that superficially marked his cheeks. A rough scrub of dark stubble rounded his face, like he hadn't shaved in a few days. Even sitting down I could tell he had at least seven inches on me.

"Want to talk about it?"

"I'm not drunk enough for that," I answered, and he just chuckled.

"Fair enough. I'm Hayden Noble," he said, extending his hand.

I took it, and a sizzle started in my toes and worked its way up as his warm hand wrapped around mine. "Juliet Banks." I pulled back quickly, guilt flooding me. I knew it had been three months, but it still felt too soon to be attracted to someone else. I wasn't blind, though. Hayden was chiseled perfection if ever I'd seen it.

"What do you do for work, Juliet Banks?"

"Nothing exciting, I'm afraid. I work for an investment

firm maintaining existing files."

He propped his elbow up on the bar and planted his chin in his hand.

"What do you do for fun?" he asked, seeming truly interested.

"Also, not exciting. I mostly read and go out for drinks with my best friend." I was embarrassed by how boring I was. It had gotten even worse over the past few months. I hadn't really wanted to do much of anything lately other than go to work, come home, and crash. Not that I was much more exciting before Drake's death, but now I had to be the most boring person on Earth.

I waved down the bartender for another drink and turned my eyes back to Hayden. As gorgeous as he was, there was an undercurrent of danger telling me to watch out. He was wearing dark-washed jeans and a black pullover sweater with black high-tops. He wasn't safe, not like Drake had been. Everything about Hayden told me he was a by-the-seat-of-his-pants kind of guy, and I had absolutely no idea what to do with someone like that.

"What about you?" I finally asked. "What do you do for work?"

"I dabble in all different things. An eloquent way of saying I don't stick around in one job for too long. Before coming to America, I worked on a fishing boat and before that I was a survivalist guide. Life is all about fulfillment and excitement, wouldn't you say?"

I couldn't agree. I'd played things safe my entire life. While it wasn't very fulfilling, it always got me through. Still, I found myself nodding as if in a trance.

"And for fun?"

A grin spread across his face, highlighting those perfect dimples. "I play just as hard as I work, love. Everything from fucking to flying."

I nearly choked on my drink. Had he really just said that?

I said nothing for a few moments, trying to compose myself. I wasn't about to talk sex with a total stranger, no matter how attractive that stranger was. It had been nearly four years since my last partner. Drake was going to correct that on his visit, and I'd been eager for it, but life had other plans. I was starting to think maybe fate was looking me in the eye and saying *Here's a sign! You're meant to be alone forever!*

I cast my gaze to Hayden, who had a perma-smile on his face and this dark, seductive aura about him. He was everything Drake wasn't, and yet I was still drawn to him. But I couldn't. It was too soon to be moving on. I'd known Drake for a year, had fallen in love with him after a couple of months. I should probably give it a little longer before I even glanced at another man.

"What's on your mind, Juliet?" Hayden asked then, pulling me out of my head and planting me back onto my stool.

"Nothing at all." I blushed. There was no way I was going to tell him I was comparing him to my dead boyfriend.

Hayden took my now empty glass and passed it to the bartender. I don't remember drinking it, but I must have. My head was fuzzy in that blissfully dull way, numbing me to my feelings and pain.

The bartender made another and sent it my way. I hadn't planned on getting drunk tonight, but I was just liberated enough by the flow of alcohol in my blood to think maybe getting drunk wasn't the worst idea I'd ever had. If it made me stop feeling hurt and ravaged by grief, even for a little while, then it couldn't be the worst thing.

"You look very dressed up for a pub," Hayden pointed out as his gaze raked over my body.

My floor-length sleeveless plum dress was made of satin, and I'd chosen black suede heels. I still had my faux fur coat on because it had been so cold outside, but I was feeling warm from the whiskey.

"I was at a work party next door," I answered with a shrug.

"And why leave a fancy party to sit alone in a pub all night?"

I hesitated, unsure if I should answer, but the alcohol was making me bolder than usual, so I told the truth. "It was a little too much for me. Too many people, too noisy. I-I haven't had the best time lately and I just wasn't ready for a party, I guess."

Hayden regarded me quietly, leaning in. "What's been going on?"

"I'm not drunk enough to tell you that," I repeated, and he threw his head back and laughed.

"Then I guess we better keep drinking."

Three Manhattans later, and I was seeing double. I felt good, better than I had in a while. It was as if all my troubles and sorrow were put on hold just so I could enjoy this moment. Hayden had been keeping me company, and he wasn't bad company to have. He'd made me smile and laugh more than once tonight, two things that I was finding difficult to do anymore since Drake's passing.

We were standing—I was mostly wobbling—next to a pool table in the back of the bar. I clung to my pool cue for balance, afraid the thing would snap under my weight. I was short with soft curves, but I wasn't sure how strongly made a cheap bar pool cue really was.

Hayden bent over the table to line up a shot. I marveled at the way his muscles involuntarily flexed beneath his sweater with every move he made. He glanced up at me and caught me looking, so I averted my eyes, my cheeks going up in flames. From the corner of my eye, I saw him pull the cue back and take a shot. The clattering of pool ball against pool ball and the telltale *thunk* of a ball being sunk into a pocket told me that Hayden was no pool amateur.

He straightened up and shot me a smile.

I smiled back and admitted, "I have no idea what I'm doing."

"You use the stick to hit the balls, simple enough."

I rolled my eyes and pointed the stick at the table only for him to laugh.

"Okay, okay, let me help you." Coming around to my side of the table, Hayden positioned himself behind me to readjust how I was holding the cue.

I held my breath while his arms came around me and gripped my fingers around the stick. He was far too close, so close I could smell him. He smelled like mint and fresh soap, a sublime combination.

"Okay, you want to hold it right for starters. You're holding it like it's a spear and you're about to stab somebody with it. You want to hold it more like this." He positioned my hands where they belonged and patted my arm. "And now you choose which ball you want to sink."

I looked around the table and pointed at a solid orange marked five. "That one." It was close enough to a pocket that I thought I could handle it.

"Okay, now it's time to line up your shot."

He slanted into my back gently to bend me forward, and all the air deflated from my lungs. He hung over me and instructed me on how to hold the cue on the table, and to make sure I was focusing my eye on the ball, but I was having trouble listening. I could only focus on his chest curved along my back.

"Are you listening, Juliet?"

"What? Yes, of course I'm listening." I shook my foggy head and refocused on the table. I lined up the shot, drew back, and knocked the white pool ball forward. I watched it roll across the table and hit the solid orange I'd had my eye on. The force of the hit encouraged the orange ball to go rolling, moving closer to the corner pocket. But it stopped just before the pocket, and I let out a sound of frustration.

"Not bad for a first try," Hayden said as he moved back and went to the other side of the table.

With him out of my space, taking his delicious scent with him, I tried thinking more clearly. Which was easier said than done, considering I was very drunk and swaying on my feet.

"You just need to put a little more force behind it."

"Story of my life," I muttered, and he raised an eyebrow with a half-smile. I waved off his impending questions and refocused on the table.

"So, are you drunk enough to tell me your life story?" he asked.

I glanced up at him expecting him to still be smiling, but he was serious, as if he wanted nothing more than to know everything about me. That heat in his eyes stripped me bare, leaving all my cards out on the table. All he had to do was flip them over to find out everything about me.

"There isn't really much to tell," I answered, glancing away from him and pretending to examine the pool table for my next shot. "My parents died when I was seven, car accident. I went to nursing school and graduated, but by the time I finished it wasn't what I wanted to do anymore. So now I type up reports for an investment company Monday through Friday, nine to five. My best friend, Morgan, works in the same building—she's the one who got me the job. And my boyfriend died in a car accident three months ago." My throat thickened with emotion by the time I finished talking. I didn't dare peek at Hayden, but I could feel his eyes on me.

Finally, he said, "Who raised you?"

I was thankful that he'd ignored the dead boyfriend bit.

"I was in and out of foster homes. My parents were the

only family I had other than an uncle who didn't want me." I just shrugged it off like it was no big deal, but as a seven-year-old child, it had crushed me. I'd always liked Uncle James and I still remember freshly the betrayal I'd felt when he'd turned me over to the state rather than take me in himself. I thought of just how disappointed and hurt my dad would have been to know that he hadn't helped me when I really needed somebody. I hadn't talked to Uncle James in years.

"Sounds rough."

"It's seriously fine. I made my own way, and that's the way I like it," I slurred.

Hayden took his next shot, sinking another ball into a pocket.

"And your boyfriend, how long were you together?"

Ah, there it was.

I deflated a little. When people found out that we hadn't even met yet, they usually seemed less sympathetic about it. "A year, more or less. He lived in London and he was days away from coming here for a visit when it happened. We hadn't, uh, we hadn't actually met in person yet."

"That doesn't really matter, though, does it? You had a connection. Which is more than most people get in this life."

I was a little surprised by his response. I hadn't expected understanding when people who actually knew me were less than compassionate about it. Who was this guy?

"What about you? You know about me, but I don't know much about you."

He seemed a little uncomfortable, but he still answered. "My mum also died when I was young, never knew my dad. She was mugged at a railway station on her way home from a trip to visit my grandparents. I was ten, and my brother was six. We had different dads, but his had walked away the minute my mum told him she was pregnant. My grandparents took us in, but our grandfather was a bastard once my grandmother passed. I ran away from home at sixteen, and I don't think my brother ever forgave me for it. Not that I could really blame him. I left him alone and that I will always regret. I didn't go to school or anything of the sort, I just found odd jobs, any way to survive. I joined an underground boxing club where I made enough money to save up, and I eventually got my brother away from our grandfather. But by that time, I was addicted to fighting and I kept doing it. My brother patched me up on more than one occasion. I made sure my brother went to school, though. He really made something of himself." He set his mouth in a firm line and scrutinized his boots.

"And what are you doing in America now" I asked, enraptured with his story. Truthfully, I hadn't expected him to be so forthcoming, though I wasn't complaining. Having someone open themselves to me was refreshing, and it stopped me from thinking about my own problems for the moment.

"I'm visiting for now, but I'm finding I rather enjoy it here. I might stay in the end, we'll see."

He stared at me across the table, his dark gaze roaming my face as if in search of something. A strong heat flourished inside me as he assessed me.

"I'll go get us some more drinks," he said.

He walked off and left me standing there contemplating his story. It was no less sad than mine, but he had someone in his corner—his brother. I had no one. I had always dreamed of having a sibling, but my parents only wanted me. I used to beg for a little brother or sister, but it never seemed to matter. My parents were happy with it being just the three of us.

When Hayden returned, he passed my drink to me, our fingers brushing. A little thrill ran through me, and I tried to stamp it down. Hayden was being nice, but he was trouble — changing jobs like I changed underwear, and illegal underground fighting. It was all exciting, but it was a new kind of danger that I would be smart not to fix myself to.

"Your turn," he said.

I took a long sip of my drink before taking my next shot. This time, the ball rolled right into the pocket. I clapped for myself and did a little dance, and Hayden laughed.

We talked about his odd jobs, my creepy boss, and our families before the accidents for the next two hours while we played game after game of pool. I wanted to play darts, but Hayden vetoed it since I could barely stand up straight.

I vaguely remembered shrugging my coat back on, though I didn't even remember taking it off, and Hayden leading me toward the exit. When we stepped out into the cold night air, I inhaled deeply, letting the chill burn my lungs. Hayden led me forward to a cab that was waiting by the curb. I thought he'd bundle me up into it and send me on my way, but to my surprise, he slid in next to me. I gave the driver my address, and we drove off.

I fell back against the seat, giggling for no good reason. I chalked it up to being as drunk as I'd ever been. Hayden smiled down at me and reached over to buckle me up. His arms came across me, his arm brushing my chest, and my stomach tightened painfully. I was so very aware of him, his scent, his proximity. It was clouding my head with desire, and that same guilt sucker-punched me right in the face. Drake was barely in the ground, and my body was already strung tight with want of another man.

I pushed it all from my head and settled my forehead on the window while the car wove through traffic. Ten minutes later I paid the taxi and tumbled out of the car onto the sidewalk in front of my building. I glared up at the stairs, wobbling and looming before me, and knew there was no way I was climbing them without breaking my neck.

"Which floor's yours?"

I turned to Hayden and pointed upward. "Third floor." I moved forward and clung to the railing, trying to push myself up the stairs.

Hayden chuckled and wrapped his arm around my waist. "Here, I'll help you."

He propelled me up the stairs, one step at a time, until finally we reached my door. I fumbled in my clutch purse for my keys and closed one eye to focus so I could put it in the lock. I cursed when my keys slipped from my fingers and hit the concrete landing.

Hayden picked them up and easily slid the key in, twisting the lock open. I had a feeling he was nowhere near as drunk as I was. I mumbled a thank you and went inside. Feeling Hayden behind me, I heard the door close, and I turned to him and nearly fell over I was so drunk. He righted me and brushed a curl from my face. I stared up at him, right into his onyx eyes, and knew I wanted this to happen. I would worry about the remorse tomorrow.

I took his hand and pulled him toward my bedroom before I could change my mind. Along the way I kicked off my shoes, reaching behind me to unzip my dress. When we entered my room, I turned to him and let the dress pool at my feet. He scrubbed a hand down his face and cleared his throat. I moved toward him and placed a hand on his chest, feeling his heart beating rapidly.

"Kiss me," I begged him.

He placed a hand on each of my shoulders and pushed me back. My brows came together, and I tilted my head to the side in confusion.

"You're drunk, Juliet," he said simply.

"Of course I am. Does that change anything?"

"Yes. I'm not going to sleep with you while you can't

make rational decisions. Give me your phone."

I shakily grabbed my purse up from the floor and found my phone, passing it to him.

He typed away on it then handed it back to me. "Now you have my number. If you still want to speak to me when you're sober, maybe we can go from there."

I felt mortified. I was throwing myself at him, and he was turning me down. All because I'd had too much to drink. But he hadn't said he didn't want it. He'd given me his number in case I felt the same way the next day. That meant he was interested to some degree, right?

Peering down at my phone, I saw his name and phone number saved on the screen. I tossed the phone on my bedside table and sighed. He was right. If I did this now, I might regret it. It was something I needed to think through, as much as I didn't want to. I was always thinking, always letting my brain rule over everything. For once I wanted to just feel something other than that desolate sadness that consumed me.

"Let's get you to bed." He was careful not to glance at my partially naked body clad only in a strapless bra and panties, leading me to my bed. Once I was tucked beneath the covers, he sat on the edge and regarded me. "You deserve better than someone who will just take you home drunk to fuck you and forget about you."

I snorted and rolled my eyes. "Maybe that's what I want, have you considered that?"

"I'm willing to bet you've never had a one-night stand before. Am I right?"

I averted my eyes, my face heating up under his gaze.

"Just as I thought."

"Does it matter if I have or not?" I snapped. "What if it's what I want now?"

"I don't think that's what you want, love," he said softly.

"I think you want someone to take the pain away, even for a moment, but this will only make it worse in the morning."

"Okay," I whispered. Of course he was right again.

"Go to sleep," he commanded.

I closed my eyes. The bed shifted as he stood, and I drifted off to the sounds of his footfalls scattering across the wooden floors.

CHAPTER THREE

The light was strong, blinding, and my head felt like it was caving in on itself. I groaned and threw the blankets over my face. The night before flashed by in snippets. I'd gone to the work party, left to go to the bar, Hayden, coming home and throwing myself at him.

I jolted upright and looked around, but I was alone. On my nightstand there was a slip of paper, a glass of water, and two pills. I quickly swallowed the pills down with a gulp of water and picked up the note.

Left you some medicine and water for your impending hango-ver. You have my number — in case you've forgotten last night. Call me sometime if you want.
Hayden

I groaned in shame. I *hadn't* forgotten. I could clearly re-call every last detail of the night before, though it was like watching it through someone else's eyes. And there, crush-ing me beneath its weight, was that guilt I'd been prepared for. Without a second thought, I'd been ready and willing to jump into bed with a man I didn't know last night while I should have still been grieving for Drake. Morgan had been telling me for two months that it was time to move on, but it felt too soon. It would always feel too soon. I would never fully get over him.

I looked at the clock — thirteen past nine. I had forty-five minutes to shower and get dressed for brunch with Morgan.

I scrambled from the bed, and nausea hit me like a crashing wave. I rushed to the bathroom to empty my stomach, holding my hair back from my face. Wrung out, I gathered up my clothes and towel and hopped in the shower.

Thirty minutes later I was dressed and ready to go, though all I wanted was to stay in bed all day. I knew Morgan. It always started off as brunch, but then she'd rope me into going shopping with her, too, and I'd oblige. I was a good friend like that.

The sound of her car's horn had me pulling on a pair of ballet flats and rushing out the door, slinging my purse over my shoulder.

"You don't seem like you had the best night," she said when I climbed in and closed the door.

I was every bit of hungover, but I thought I'd covered up the worst of it with some makeup. My hair was being an unruly mess today, so I'd braided it down my back, though little sprigs of curls managed to escape still.

"What happened to you?"

"I went by a bar on my way home last night," I answered nonchalantly, as if going to a bar alone was something I often did.

"And?" She could sense there was more to the story, and I knew she wouldn't drop it.

"And I met someone who made sure I got home safely, where I went to bed and woke up with a hangover. There, happy?"

She was surprised, but her expression quickly vanished to make way for a conspiratorial smile. "You met someone? And he took you home? Did my girl finally hit her first homerun in years?" she belted out in a singsong.

"No, it wasn't like that. He just put me to bed and told me to go to sleep." I was grouchy from the hangover and embarrassed that I'd made a fool of myself last night.

Morgan huffed and backed out of the parking spot in front of my building. "Well, that's boring. Why did nothing else happen?"

"He said I was too drunk," I grumbled unwillingly. I didn't want anyone to know what an idiot I'd made of myself, not even Morgan.

"So you were planning on something happening?"

I shoved my sunglasses onto my face and kept my focus on the scenery outside the windshield. "I don't know what I was thinking. I'm not ready for something like that." My voice got softer as I said, "No matter where I go, I see Drake in everything. He even had an English accent like Drake."

Morgan was quiet a moment, choosing her words wisely. "I think it's normal that you might see him in things, but I think it's also important that you don't let it control your life either, Juliet. He would want you to be happy, and right now, I don't think you're happy."

"I'm perfectly fine with the way things are," I protested, but it was halfhearted. I wasn't perfectly fine. I was wallowing in sadness over the missed opportunity I'd had with Drake.

"If you say so," she muttered, though we both knew she didn't mean it.

Twenty minutes later we were outside a small corner bistro downtown. It was busy, as per usual for a Sunday morning, so we sat off to the side in hopes that a table would open up soon. While we sat there on a bench, Morgan told me all about the party. It apparently got very out of hand toward the end with everyone drunk on champagne. The party got shut down when one of the girls from the fifth floor tried to flash her boobs on the stage. I laughed, almost sorry I'd missed it.

When a hostess called our names, we stood from the bench outside and followed her to a little table outside.

"You don't have any inside?" Morgan asked her, and the hostess shook her head.

"We have heat lamps out here on the patio, so you'll hardly tell the difference," the hostess chirped, brightly smiling.

Morgan mumbled something and took a seat, so I followed suit. With our menus splayed open in front of us, Morgan kept going on about the party and how she and Mark had slipped off into an unoccupied room to have sex.

"Weren't you worried someone would catch you?" I was shocked that she'd be so risky, but she just smiled smugly.

"That's what makes it exciting, my dear," she answered, winking devilishly.

The waitress came and took our orders, also bringing us some coffee. Coffee and something to settle my stomach was exactly what I needed to cure this hangover. My head throbbed, probably due to throwing up the only medicine I'd taken this morning.

Normally I loved Morgan's stories, and I lived vicariously through them, but today they were leaving me feeling frustrated. I should be grateful Hayden hadn't taken advantage of the situation—it said a lot about him—but I felt like I was crawling out of my skin any time I let my mind drift toward him. And I thought of him a lot. He was different than anything I ever dreamed I wanted or was attracted to, yet here I was wondering what his skin tasted like and if he liked to talk dirty during sex. Then that led to more guilt piling up at my feet.

I needed to get him out of my head once and for all. I'd delete his number and move on with life. He'd been nice to me when I'd needed it, that was what fueled my attraction. Nothing more, nothing less.

"So, tell me more about this mystery guy you met last night."

I looked up from my cup of coffee and gave Morgan a pointed stare. "There isn't much to tell. He was nice, but he's definitely not my type. Too . . . wild." It was the only word I could think to describe him. Where Drake was reserved and gentle, I knew just by the way Hayden carried himself that he was rough around the edges.

"Ooh, a bad boy. Every girl needs one of those in their life." Morgan's eyes lit up.

I shot her down. "Not going to happen. I'm deleting his number first chance I get."

"No! Don't do that. He might be what you need to get yourself out of this slump you're in. Just think this through before you do anything rash."

The thing was, all I'd done since meeting Hayden last night was think, and I was still coming up empty. I could admit I was attracted to him as much as it triggered feelings of betraying Drake in me, but Hayden also scared me. He represented something untamed that I hadn't strayed toward once my whole life. Even when I was bounced around from home to home as a child and saw things no child should ever see, I never once thought about going down those paths myself.

"It would be a mistake," I said, trying to end the conversation.

"What does he look like?"

"Tall, really tall. Black hair, really dark-brown eyes. And he was definitely in shape." I thought back to the way his muscles had rippled as he'd moved across the pool table, peeking up at me through his lashes.

"Oh okay, sort of like that guy over there?"

I jerked my head up from my cup and swung my head around. Sure enough, Hayden was sitting at a table just inside, and he was smiling at me. I turned away quickly, but not before seeing him get up from the table. What was he doing here? In all the places he could be in this city, he just had to be at this one bistro.

"Incoming!"

"Juliet," he purred, and I craned my neck up to see him standing over me.

"Hayden," I responded.

"What are the chances?" He threw himself down on the chair next to me and reclined back, stretching his legs out in front of him. I was convinced the man could make himself comfortable and at home no matter where he was. I cast a glance at Morgan who nodded toward Hayden and mouthed, *say something!*

"Indeed," I said lamely. "What brings you here?"

"I'm staying not too far away, and my friend said this was a good place for breakfast." He finally glanced away from me to acknowledge Morgan. Holding out his hand he said, "Hayden Noble."

"Morgan Russo," she answered, shaking his hand.

I felt a stab of jealousy that she was getting to touch him before I shook myself internally and told myself to calm down. Hayden's eyes came to me again, and I found myself examining them. They were so dark I could hardly distinguish the iris from pupil even in the sun. They were beautiful in their own way. Not clear like the sky or stormy blue like the ocean, but dark like coal and burning just as hot.

"How are you feeling today? You were very drunk last night."

I didn't need the reminder. I currently felt like I'd been flattened by a tractor trailer. "Just peachy," I said, regardless of how I was truly feeling.

"She mentioned that you took her home and put her to bed. Thanks for watching out for her," Morgan interjected.

I shot her a dirty glare. I didn't want him knowing I'd been talking about him. That would only encourage him, if he was inclined to have anything to do with me in the first place.

Hayden shrugged lazily and said, "It wasn't the worst night I've ever had." He winked at me, and a dimple creased his cheek as his mouth lifted to one side.

I blushed, focusing my attention down into my cup and picked at invisible lint on my pants.

"Well, I know Juliet would just love to see you again sometime, right, Juliet?" She kicked me under the table.

I gave her another dirty look.

She kicked me again, and I yelped.

"Okay, fine, yes. I'd love to."

Hayden raised a dark eyebrow and bent forward. "Tomorrow night, eight o'clock."

"What happens tomorrow night" I asked breathlessly, almost unwilling to believe I was doing this.

"That's a surprise, love. Are you in?"

I nodded carefully. He was inches from my face, and that distinct soapy mint smell came rolling off him. Was it even possible for someone to smell so delectable?

"Great, I'll pick you up at eight then," he said.

"What should I wear?" I asked, watching him stand.

He raked his gaze over me slowly, and I didn't miss that it lingered on my chest. For all the things I hated about my body, my boobs weren't one of them. They were big enough without being unmanageable.

"What you're wearing now is fine," he said.

"So I should just dress normally then?"

"Yes, normally. No frilly dresses needed," he joked.

I cracked a smile in spite of the nerves swimming around in my gut.

"I'll see you tomorrow." He smiled and threw his hand up as a goodbye.

I watched him stalk off. Even the way he moved exuded

confidence. I gave him one last longing stare while he walked back inside in more dark jeans and black boots, a deep-red shirt with a black leather jacket over it, and a black beanie pulled down over his ears. It was so far from what I'd normally go after, yet here I was accepting a date.

A *date*. What was I doing? I couldn't go on a date with him.

"Ho-ly shit, you didn't tell me he was gorgeous!" Morgan stared after him, too, shaking her head.

"Is he? I hadn't noticed," I said casually.

Morgan rolled her eyes. "Yeah, okay, let's just say I believe you. Why aren't you throwing yourself at him?"

I technically had, and he'd turned me down. My confidence wasn't at an all-time high at the moment, though I knew Hayden had done it for my own good. I did appreciate it, truly. He'd been right. If I'd slept with him last night, then I would have definitely regretted it this morning.

"Because not everything is about how someone looks, Morgan. Besides, have you actually given him a once-over? Something about him is setting off all my red flags."

"Uh, yeah, he's the very definition of a bad boy. I can see trouble coming off him from a mile away. That just makes it all the more exciting, though. You're in for a treat. The last guy like him that I was with was excellent in bed. Probably the best I've ever had, if I'm being honest." She got a far-off dreaminess in her eye as she reminisced over her past lover.

"He freaks me out," I stated then took a sip of my coffee.

"All the more reason to give it a chance. When have you ever taken a risk?"

Truthfully, I considered falling in love with someone in a different country risk enough, and I saw where that had gotten me. "I already agreed to the date, you can stop trying to talk me up," I pointed out.

"Yeah, you agreed to it, but I can see that you aren't really feeling it, and I want to know why. An extremely gorgeous man wants to take you out on a date that may or may not end in amazing sex. Why are you so unenthused about it?"

I took a deep breath, then sighed. "It still feels like I'm betraying Drake. I know he's gone and there's nothing I can do about it, but it feels too soon to be moving on to someone else already. It makes me feel like the worst kind of person to hop into someone else's bed when I never even had the chance to be in his."

Morgan studied me sympathetically but determined. "Drake would want you to be happy, sweetie, and I think you could be if you'd just let yourself. There's nothing wrong with living. The world didn't stop going on once he died, so your world shouldn't stop either. The accident wasn't your fault, but you're taking it on yourself, and it isn't healthy."

"It's just hard, you know? I almost had him here, almost got to know what it felt like being with someone who truly loved me. And that was ripped away from me." My throat closed up, and I swallowed the lump down.

"I know, Juliet, but you're going to get past this. I'm by your side, and I'll help you through it." She squeezed my hand as the waitress appeared with our food and left.

I wasn't feeling all that hungry now between the sadness over Drake and the anxiety over my date with Hayden, but I still forced a couple of bites down. I spared a glance inside, but the table Hayden had been occupying was empty.

Morgan drove me back home, and we spent the afternoon picking out an outfit for my date, though I assured Morgan I could handle dressing myself. We settled on a cream-knit sweater with a cowl neck and dark cigarette jeans with a pair of tan knee-high boots. It was still my style without being dressed down or up too much, since I still had no clue what we were doing. I was almost worried he was going to take me to one of his illegal fighting matches but quickly pushed the idea from my head. I wasn't sure how long he'd been here, but surely it wasn't long enough to get himself into that kind of trouble.

By the time Morgan left I was starting to come off my hangover. My headache eased, and my stomach had stopped rolling since I'd gotten some food in it. I poured myself a glass of cola and settled in on the couch to watch some TV.

I stayed there all afternoon trying to distract myself from what I was in for tomorrow night, to no avail. I kept seeing these flashing images of Hayden sweeping me into his arms and kissing me. Regardless of all Morgan had said, nothing would take away the pain I felt at moving on from Drake. I wasn't sure I was ready, but there was only one way to find out. I'd go on this date with Hayden, and I'd let destiny take its course.

Chapter Four

I was sitting at my computer filling in data on a spread-sheet when a shadow fell over me. I peered up to see Carter standing there with his shark-like smile.

"Juliet, you're very lovely today."

I was wearing a gray tweed pantsuit, really nothing special. "Thank you, Mr. Dunlap. Was there something you needed from me?"

"For starters, you can just call me Carter."

I had taken to calling him by his last name only to show him that our relationship was, and always would be, of a professional capacity.

"And second, I wanted to invite you out tonight. A couple of us are going to this nightclub downtown called Club Rogue that just opened for drinks, and I was wondering if you'd be my date."

"I'm actually busy tonight, sorry." I pulled an expression of apology, though I wasn't sorry at all. He creeped me out on more than one level, and I wanted him to stop asking me to spend time with him, though I didn't feel comfortable enough to address it with him. My job was in his hands, and I couldn't afford to be jobless right now.

"Maybe next time then," he said with a tight smile.

I pursed my lips and watched him walk away. I quickly got back to work so I could finish early and go home to prepare for my date. All morning I'd been nervously biting my nails over it. What if Hayden didn't like me sober? Or worse yet, what if he *did* like me? I wasn't sure which would hurt more. Knowing I was a boring person, or that I'd have to choose between my dead boyfriend and a guy who made me tingle all over without even touching me.

I supposed I shouldn't be too nervous—he'd seen me in my underwear already. I cringed recalling the night before and how desperate I'd seemed. It would have been so easy to take me up on my offer, and he hadn't.

At four-thirty, I shut my computer down and grabbed my bag from under my desk. I walked to the elevators, getting out my phone and sending Morgan a quick message to let her know I was heading home and to wish me luck. I was going to need all the luck in the world to get through tonight. I was shaking with anticipation and fear. I found myself a little excited about it, which surprised me, but I didn't do well with unknowns, and not knowing where we were going was making me more than anxious.

You've got this xx

I smiled down at my phone reading Morgan's message and stepped onto the elevator. I'd driven to work, so I took the elevator down to the garage and picked my way through the cars until I found my little blue car.

On the drive home I listened to some self-help audiobook a woman in my office had suggested on how to deal with grief and loss. So far it was just causing irrational anger. All this talk of letting go and moving on with my life was making the situation worse, so I shut the radio off and drove the rest of the way in silence.

I climbed the two flights of stairs, then let myself into my apartment and dropped my purse off on the kitchen counter. I removed my hairclip and shook my hair loose. It was getting long, almost halfway down my back now. There was this desire to cut it off, but I knew I'd regret it if I did. It was too curly to keep short. I could easily pass as a poodle when my hair was any shorter than just at my shoulders.

I slipped my shoes off and carried them to my closet as I undressed for my shower. Finding my best scented soaps, I lined them up along the shower ledge and got in under the spray. The water was hot and helped relax me some, though my body was still thrumming with anxiety over what the night before me held. Not wanting to take any chances, I shaved and lathered myself up in soap that smelled of peonies.

When I climbed out I toweled myself off and wrung my hair dry, then changed into the outfit Morgan had helped me choose. It was seven-thirty by the time I was done with dressing and primping, and I still had thirty minutes until Hayden arrived. I paced back and forth in the living room, overthinking this whole thing. Twice I came close to calling him and telling him I'd gotten sick, though I knew he'd see through it.

In the end, a knock came at my door. I stopped dead in my tracks and stared at it. Slowly I made my way to the door and checked through the peephole, though I knew who was on the other side. I cracked the door open, and there he stood, taking up the entire doorway as he leaned against the frame. I opened the door wider, and he smiled.

"Ready to go?"

"Um, yes. Just let me grab my purse." I snatched it and my keys off the counter and turned back to the door. When I left my apartment into the February chill, I wrapped my arms around myself.

Hayden placed his hand on my lower back and steered me toward the stairs. We got to the bottom, and he headed right for a motorcycle parked in the lot. I came up short.

"What's that?"

"It's my bike," he said nonchalantly and grabbed a helmet off the back.

"I'm not getting on that thing."

He smiled and prowled toward me. He stood directly in front of me, taking my face in his hands, and tilted my head up so my gaze would lock with his.

"How did I know that one was coming? Live a little, Juliet."

"How can I live if I die in a motorcycle accident?"

He laughed and brushed his thumb across my cheek. A shiver crawled its way down my spine as he continued stroking my skin with his thumb.

"It's perfectly safe. You're going to be fine, love."

I glanced over at the motorcycle uneasily. "We can always take my vehicle," I offered. "It's the blue car over there."

"You drive a very practical car. Why am I not surprised?" He was trying to hide a smile but failed.

"Is there something wrong with driving something reliable?" I asked defensively.

"Not at all, it's just very you."

"How would you know? You don't know me."

He stroked his chin and nodded. "True, but I can determine enough from what I do know."

He was irritating me, and we'd barely even made it out of my apartment.

"Oh yeah? What determinations have you made so far? Tell me so I can shoot them down now."

He took a step closer and smiled as if this whole thing was funny to him. "If I'm right, you get on the bike."

"Fine. Go ahead."

"You're very type A and like things a certain way. The biggest risk you ever made in your life was putting all your money on a long-distance relationship. You have many acquaintances, but I'm willing to bet Morgan is your only true friend because you don't know how to trust people. Sometimes you're not even sure if you can trust yourself. Like right now. You're wondering what the fuck you were thinking by agreeing to this. Your greatest fear is letting yourself down, and your biggest dream is to feel stable enough in life to call yourself successful even though you sometimes feel like a failure for doing nothing with your nursing degree. Am I getting close?"

I glared at him and debated marching myself back inside and slamming the door in his face. In the end I just held my hand out and said, "Give me the damn helmet."

He said nothing but smiled to himself and passed the extra helmet to me. He took a moment to explain to me how to hold on and how to lean into curves in the event we came upon them, then hopped on and patted the seat behind him.

I couldn't believe I was about to do this. My heart thundered away, but I still threw my leg over the side of the motorcycle. I clung to Hayden, though we weren't even moving yet.

"It'll be fun, you'll see," he called out and started up the engine.

The bike roared to life and vibrated between my legs. It wasn't an unpleasant sensation, but it was one I wasn't sure I'd ever get used to. Rolling backward out of the parking spot, Hayden leaned forward slightly and accelerated. I screamed as we zoomed away from my building.

I clutched the front of Hayden's leather jacket, trembling in fear that we'd hit a bump and go flying at any moment. Though I was scared, I was also exhilarated. It felt so free, the openness, the wind blowing over me and caressing me like a lover. I could see why people enjoyed it. Aside from the danger of it all, it wasn't as bad as I thought it'd be.

When we pulled into a gravel parking lot on the west side of town, I was still holding on to Hayden for dear life. He removed his helmet and turned his head. "We're here."

I took off my helmet and stared. We were parked next to a

building labeled the Wayward Druid. I knew it was a music venue, though I'd never been inside. In fact, I'd never been to a concert once in my life unless you counted the time I had to pick Morgan up from an outdoor festival when she'd caught the guy she was with sticking his tongue down another girl's throat.

"We're going to a concert" I asked dumbly. Why else would we be here?

"A friend of mine's band is playing, and I told him I'd come. It seemed like more fun with company." He slipped off the motorcycle and held his hand out to help me off.

I took it, and his warmth enveloped me. My freezing hands welcomed the heat of his. To my surprise, he didn't let go as approached the doors.

He flashed two tickets at the door and slipped inside. I suddenly felt very overdressed after scanning the room. The dress code seemed very casual and laidback. Jeans, graphic tees, canvas shoes. I couldn't have been more out of place.

"I think I need to go home and change clothes," I yelled to Hayden over the music.

There was already a musician on stage plucking a guitar and crooning into the microphone.

He led me to the bar. "You look perfect," he called back to me, so I didn't argue.

At the bar we settled onto two stools that someone had just vacated and ordered drinks. I got my usual Manhattan, and Hayden chose a beer. He took a sip when our drinks were shoved in front of us and made a face.

"Beer tastes so different here. I'm still not used to it," he said, taking another sip.

"Is it really that different over there?"

"We have some of the same kinds, but most of what I've tasted over here just seems so watered down."

I wasn't much of a beer connoisseur, so I had zero input

on the subject. "That's why I just stick to whiskey. You can never go wrong with whiskey."

He gave me an adorable dimpled smile and inclined his head in agreement. "I'm not looking to get totally pissed tonight, love. One of us has to be sober enough to drive us back."

My stomach, as it did every time, clenched when he'd called me love. I knew it was a typical endearment in England, but it also felt so intimate the way he'd said it to me.

"I suppose I should also be drinking something a little lighter, then."

"Nonsense, I brought you here to have fun, and you loosen up a good bit when you're drunk. Just don't get blackout drunk and we'll be fine," he joked.

I laughed and playfully slapped his shoulder. "I was *not* blackout drunk the other night. I can remember the whole night perfectly fine," I added.

"You do, do you? So you recall demanding me to kiss you." It wasn't really a question, just a reminder that I had asked for his touch at one point. Maybe that was his way of asking permission.

"Yes, I do," I said softly, all my humor withering away. "I also recall you turning me down, so your loss, I suppose."

This time he laughed and shook his head. "The price I pay for being a gentleman. My loss indeed."

We looked at one another quietly for a moment, tension strung tight between us. I could feel it as if it were tangible, surely he could, too. I was the first to turn away, darting my gaze toward my lap as I pushed a strand of curls behind my ear.

From the corner of my eye I saw Hayden take another sip of beer, so I mimicked him and picked up my glass. I decided I wasn't going to get drunk tonight. I would have two or three drinks, but I wanted to be clearheaded. If I got drunk

I'd probably throw myself at him again, and I wouldn't be able to blame him if he took me up on it this time.

"How was work today?" he suddenly asked.

I rolled my eyes. "My boss, the one I was telling you about, asked me to go out with him tonight. Apparently this new nightclub opened up, and a couple of my colleagues were going. He wanted me to be his date. I don't know how many times I have to say no before he gets the hint that I'm not interested." Carter wouldn't get it even if I carried around a big flashing sign that said *no thanks.*

"Want me to kick his ass?"

I couldn't tell if he was joking or being serious, but his face told me he was probably being serious. "No, that's okay. He isn't worth going to jail over." I laughed, trying to lighten the mood.

"The offer still stands," he said then gulped down more beer.

I appreciated his concern, but I could handle Carter. It was annoying that he asked me out every chance he got, but he was harmless. I could deal with having to constantly turn him down.

"What about you? What did you do all day?"

"Played poker and hung out with a friend mostly. The same friend who's playing in the band tonight. He owns an autobody shop and he was having me go over a few things. I did some mechanics back in London years ago and I rebuilt the engine on my car back home myself. If there's one thing I know, it's cars."

I had to admit it, I was impressed. But the poker made me a little nervous. I imagined a back room in a dingy building with loan sharks surrounding the table under a dim light. It was probably nowhere near as exciting, but I tended to get carried away.

"How do you have friends here if you lived in London?"

"The band played a show in London one year that I attended, and their van broke down, so I helped them fix it. He moved over for a while, and we reconnected, and he just moved back here three years ago. We'd been mates for years, so he's letting me crash at his place while I'm in town. I've been here about a month now, but we picked up right where we left off. Funny how that can happen sometimes, eh?"

I wouldn't know. The only real friend I'd ever had was Morgan and I'd only known her for five years. I met her in college. She'd gone to school for business and marketing while I'd been in for nursing. We were dormmates, and it was the closest I could ever remember being to someone since my parents' deaths. She was so headstrong and determined that I latched myself to her and never let go.

"I'm sure it beats having to stay in a crappy motel or lonely hotel," I said then drank my Manhattan. "How long are you planning on staying here?"

"I'm not sure yet. It depends on how things go."

It was a vague answer, which I hadn't been expecting. Whether or not I was going to waste my energy on getting to know him on any level depended on how long he was going to be here. He could be gone next week for all I knew, and then I'd be back to square one—sitting alone in my apartment with a thundercloud over my head, jaded not just from losing my boyfriend, but from also being left by a guy who wanted me for nothing more than a week-long fling.

Applause erupted as the singer finished his last song and exited the stage.

Hayden stood and grasped my elbow. "They're about to come on. Let's go join the crowd."

Chapter Five

We were standing in the center of the crowd, plunged into total darkness when the first lines of a song were belted out and flashing lights of purple and blue lit up the stage, centering in on the band. Hayden threw his arm over my shoulder and pulled me in close. He sang the lyrics low, and I was surprised to find that his voice wasn't half bad.

The music was almost soothing, not too boisterous and mind-rattling like I'd assumed it would be. Truth be told, I had been expecting heavy metal or hard rock, but this had more of an indie feel to it. It was right up my alley.

Hayden leaned down and said into my ear, "I'm going to go get us some more drinks. Be right back."

He took my empty glass, and I watched him disappear to the bar. I turned my attention back to the stage and listened to the singer croon about missing their lover and how they'd never get them back. My mind immediately went to Drake. I wasn't sure if I believed in Heaven, but if it was there, I hoped Drake, who would definitely be looking down on me, could forgive me for going on this date with Hayden. And I hoped he'd forgive me if anything else happened.

I wasn't dead set on anything happening, but I'd prepared in case it did. I'd shaved and put on my best lotions and I'd talked myself up to be open to what could happen tonight. But I was still hung up on all the reasons why I shouldn't sleep with him. For starters, I barely knew him, and it wasn't typical of me to have sex with someone I didn't know. Then there was the not knowing how long he would

be around. And then I had that looming cloud of doubt surrounding Drake. It still felt like going behind his back even
though he wasn't around anymore.

An arm came around my waist, and a deep voice whispered in my ear, "Hey, honey, you here alone?"

I didn't know who it was, but I knew it definitely wasn't
Hayden. I tried to tear myself away, but the man just
dragged me back into his front and kept whispering in my
ear.

"Why don't we get out of here?"

"Let me go," I yelled. "Let me go or I'll gouge your eyes
out."

"Come on, baby, I'm just having some fun." The man
laughed.

"I think she said to let her go."

I whipped my head to the side. Hayden stood there with
our drinks in his hands. I pleaded to him with my eyes to
help me.

"Back the fuck off. Now."

The man immediately released me and held his hands up.
I shuffled back until I was against Hayden.

"Chill, man. I was just playing around."

"Drunk or not, I'll kick your ass if I see you do that shit to
her again." Hayden's voice was cold as he threatened the
man, and I could see that ruthlessness in him then that had
probably pressed him into the world of underground
fighting.

The man just slipped away and disappeared into the
crowd. Hayden looked down at me, to where I was huddled
up against him, and pushed his cheek into my hair.

"Are you okay?" he asked, muttering into my ear.

"Yeah, I'll be fine," I assured him with a nod. "Let's just
forget that happened."

Hayden grunted and passed my drink to me. I took a

large swallow of it to stop my legs from shaking and tried to smile. The song ended then, and the singer started talking to the crowd.

To distract Hayden, I leaned over and asked, "Which one is your friend?"

"The drummer. His name is Berkley."

He pointed to the drummer, a lean, thin man. He looked young, even younger than me, and he had long, light-brown hair pulled back from his face. He was adorable in a younger brother kind of way.

When the next song started, this one slower than the rest, Hayden gathered me into his arms and swayed with me. I was feeling tipsy, the alcohol just starting to hit me. I laid my head on his chest, and his heart beat fast. Was he as nervous as I was? If so, he hid it much better than I did.

Tonight he smelled like a fresh shower, and that faint mint lingered around me. I closed my eyes and let him lead the way in our soft sway. After a moment I drew back some and lifted my head. He stared down into my eyes, desire flooding them. I knew he wanted me, and if there was any doubt, the expression on his face now confirmed it. I gulped hard.

He lowered his mouth to my ear and whispered, "I really want to kiss you right now."

A shiver rocked my body as he held me close. He nuzzled the skin just below my ear, the prickle of his stubble rubbing my skin in a way that had my toes curling in my boots. Then a featherlight kiss right at my throat drew a soft moan from me. Hayden leaned back and watched me. I bit my bottom lip under the intensity of his gaze.

He bent his neck and pressed his forehead to mine, our eyes locking. The lightest brush of his lips sent my spine rigid. I wasn't ready for this. I backed out of his arms and stammered, "I-I, um, I'm sorry. I need to go to the restroom."

I pushed my way through the crowd and ran straight for the bathroom. The music was muffled once the door was closed behind me, and I headed straight for the sink. I gripped the edges of the counter and drew in a deep breath. What was I doing and who was I kidding? This was a horrible idea. It was too soon, and I wasn't ready to move on to someone else. Tears filled my eyes, and I tried hard to blink them away.

A knock came on the bathroom door, and I opened it just a crack.

"Come out, love. I won't try to kiss you again, I promise," Hayden said.

He didn't have his usual playful smile on his face, so I knew he was actually being serious. I grabbed my drink up from the counter and downed the whole thing before stepping outside the bathroom. I focused on my feet in embarrassment, but his fingers came up under my chin and pushed my head up so our eyes met.

"You aren't ready for that, and that's okay. I'm a patient man."

"You aren't . . . mad?"

He snorted and said, "Only an asshole would be mad that you aren't ready for intimacy."

I exhaled in relief, and when he held his hand out, I took it.

"The concert's almost over. Berkley wants us to meet him backstage if that's cool with you."

"Yeah, that's fine," I answered. I couldn't really explain how I was feeling. I knew I wasn't ready for kissing and sex, but I also didn't want the night to end. As much as it killed me to admit it, I did actually enjoy Hayden's company.

Hayden dragged me toward the stage doors, where a bouncer stood. He said something to the bouncer, and he stepped aside to let us by. Hayden pushed open the door and guided me through. Backstage a few people milled about or lounged on chairs. There was even a whole separate bar back there. We went to a worn lime-green couch, and Hayden pulled me down to sit with him. He put his arm around me and held me close. That I didn't mind so much.

"Is this okay?" he murmured in my ear.

I nodded.

When the lead singer told the crowd goodnight and they filed in off the stage into the backstage area, they all headed for the bar. Berkley caught sight of Hayden and headed over with a smile. Hayden stood and yanked him into a hug.

"Thanks for coming, man. Did you like the show?"

"Excellent as usual," Hayden replied, his dimpled smile surfacing. "I want you to meet someone. Berkley, this is Juliet. Juliet, this is my mate Berkley."

I stood and held my hand out, but Berkley just wrapped me up in a friendly hug.

"Nice to meet you, Juliet. Are you two a thing? If not, I wouldn't mind getting your number." He waggled his eyebrows at me.

I burst out laughing.

"Berkley," Hayden warned, which only had me laughing harder.

"It was a joke, H. You know I would never encroach." Berkley shot me a knowing smile.

I smiled back. I decided then that I really liked Berkley.

"I'm going to get a drink," he said, "but I'll be back."

Berkley headed to the bar, and we settled back into the couch. When Hayden put his arm around me again, I snuggled deeper into him. This much I could handle—it was the other stuff that felt too far beyond my reach for now.

"What do you think?"

"Of the music or Berkley?" I asked.

"Both."

"Hm, well, the music was really nice. I wasn't expecting such chill music, honestly, but I liked it a lot. And Berkley seems sweet. Like the little brother I never had."

Hayden barked out a laugh and held me tighter against him. "Good, wouldn't want to have to fight my one good mate over you. I won't tell him you called him brother material, though. Might bruise his ego."

We smiled at one another, and Berkley threw himself down into a chair in front of us.

"So, how did you two meet?" he asked then took a swig of his beer.

"At a bar," I answered. "I left a work party early, and we ended up getting drunk together, playing pool. Well, mostly he played pool and I pretended I knew what I was doing."

"All great love stories happen over booze and pool," Berkley said, winking.

My face must have been red as a beet, so I cleared my throat.

"Were you able to get that car up and running?" Hayden asked him, smoothly changing the subject.

Berkley went into a story about how he'd replaced this part and that and finally got the car running and that he wouldn't have been able to do it without Hayden's guidance. They talked for a while about cars and guy stuff. I tried to hide my yawn, but Hayden saw me.

"We're going to get going. This one has to be up early for work tomorrow."

"All right, man, I'll see you back at the house later? Or maybe I won't," Berkley teased, the three of us standing to give goodbyes.

"You'll see me later," Hayden promised.

They hugged, and Berkley also leaned in to give me a quick hug as well. Hayden took my hand and led me back through the stage door, into the mostly empty venue, then out into the parking lot. We climbed onto his motorcycle, putting our helmets on. I wrapped my arms around his waist, and Hayden started it up and we zipped away.

I wasn't as freaked out this time around and actually almost enjoyed it. Laying my head on his back, I closed my eyes and listened to the wind rip past. We came to a stop, and I sat up straight and looked around. We were already at my apartment building. I slid off the bike after he climbed off and removed the helmet, setting it down on the seat.

Hayden walked me upstairs to my door, where we stood quietly watching one another. He took a step closer to me and held me close. "Thank you for coming with me tonight, love."

"Thanks for inviting me. I had a lot of fun." I meant it, too. I hadn't expected to enjoy myself so much, but it had been something I'd really needed whether he knew it or not. But we needed to address the elephant in the room. "I'm really sorry I got so weird back there."

"You don't have to apologize. If anything, I should. I forget not everyone moves as fast as I do." He smiled down at me sweetly.

"It isn't your fault I'm so screwed up." I laughed humorlessly.

He swept my hair from my face and stroked my cheek. "You aren't screwed up. Whatever your hang-up is, I can wait for you to deal with it. Like I said, I can be very patient when I need to be. And I'm willing to wait."

His words instilled some confidence in me, so I reached up and kissed him on the cheek.

"Thank you, Hayden," I whispered.

He put his hand around my neck and pressed my head to his chest, resting his cheek on my hair.

"You're going to be the death of me, Juliet Banks. I just

know it."

I didn't understand what he meant by that, but I didn't ask. I felt emotional enough by the events of the night, so I didn't want to delve any further into my feelings.

"Should I give you my number now in case you want to drag me to another concert?" I asked the question even though my stomach lurched. What if he didn't really want to see me again and was just being nice? I wasn't a sure thing like I was positive he was used to. Morgan was right, he was absolutely gorgeous, and there was no reason he had to stick around me when he could easily go out and find someone who would give him what he needed right this minute.

"Absolutely. I'm going bowling with Berkley and some other friends later this week. You're welcome to come if you're interested."

I smiled up at him, relieved he still wanted to be around me.

"I'd love to," I answered as I rattled off my phone number while he put it into his phone.

I let out another yawn, and Hayden picked up my hand, laying a sweet kiss along the back.

"Goodnight, Juliet."

"Goodnight." I let myself into the apartment and watched him disappear down the stairs through a crack in the door. I went to my room and undressed to the sound of his motorcycle starting up then speeding away.

I played the whole night over in my head as I got into bed and stared at my ceiling. Hayden dressed and had the demeanor of what Morgan had dubbed a bad boy, but he'd been nothing short of perfect tonight. He'd treated me with kindness and respect, just like he had that night he'd brought me home from the bar.

It was possible that although he was involved in activities that I'd probably consider unsavory, there was a truly good, decent person beneath all of that hard exterior. He'd lowered his guard some by showing that to me, and I'd repaid him by throwing my walls up so high he had no hope of jumping them. I wondered then if he'd go off and try to find someone else to sleep with tonight. If he went back to the music venue to hang out some more with Berkley, he was sure to find someone. I didn't like how that made me feel, though, so I tried to push it from my mind.

Hayden hadn't seemed upset or disappointed when I'd backed away from his kiss. He'd seemed understanding, like he knew what I was going through. I'd told him a few things about Drake that night at the bar, and he'd looked sad. Maybe it reminded him of something, or maybe he just felt sorry for me. I didn't know, but I did know he was multifaceted. Every time I thought I had him figured out some, a new side of him appeared that threw me for a loop all over again.

I also couldn't deny that I was frustrated. Sexually frustrated. My mind and heart weren't ready to move past Drake, but my body told a different story. I was humming with tension, my panties damp as scenes of Hayden kissing me and touching me played about in my head. Rolling over to my bedside table, I opened the drawer and took out my vibrator.

For the first time in over a year, I touched myself to images of someone other than Drake. When I was done and utterly spent, I closed my eyes and whispered into the air, "I'm sorry, Drake. Please forgive me."

The air didn't speak out and it couldn't, because Drake was dead and gone. And maybe I was just now starting to realize what that meant.

Chapter Six

The workday was long, and I found myself checking my phone constantly to see if Hayden had messaged me, but he hadn't. That niggling doubt in the back of my mind was telling me I wouldn't hear from him again. I was sure I'd blown it. Then the more rational part of me tried to whip that voice into submission by reminding me that it hadn't even been twenty-four hours yet. Wasn't there some rule about when to call back after a date? Maybe he was going by that, and that's why I hadn't heard from him.

I'd taken a cab to work that morning, since my car was stalling, but Morgan offered to drive me home, so I took the elevator down to the garage and waited by her car for her. When the click of her heels echoed in the garage, I turned to watch her hurry over.

We were barely in the car before she bombarded me with questions. "So, how did it go? Are you going to see each other again? Did you sleep with him? If you did you have to tell me if he's as much a god in bed as I assume he is."

"Slow down, Morgan." I laughed. "No, we didn't sleep together. He was actually very much a gentleman last night." She seemed disappointed. "But he did invite me to go bowling with him and his friends later this week."

"So you're going on another date! That's a good thing. That means he's in this for more than just the sex."

I hoped she was right. I wasn't really one for meaningless sex, which was why I'd never had a one-night stand as Hayden had so correctly guessed.

Still, I didn't want to get ahead of myself. It was very possible he just wanted to be friends now after I'd turned down his kiss. "He tried to kiss me, and I freaked out and ran off to the bathroom."

"You did *what*?" Morgan slammed her foot on the brake as we backed from the parking spot and gaped at me. "Why would you do that?"

"I . . . I don't know. I guess I just wasn't ready for it yet. I'm still trying to navigate this whole dating thing and I feel like I'm failing miserably at it." There wasn't a doubt in my mind that if I'd kissed him back last night that the night would have gone much differently. I did want it, I wanted him, but I couldn't set aside the feelings of disloyalty to Drake long enough to follow through.

"Well, how did he react?"

She put the car into gear, and we drove up to the gate arm that kept us trapped inside the garage. Morgan punched in a few numbers on a mounted keypad, and the arm lifted to let us through.

"He was very understanding, which I hadn't expected. He said he understood that I wasn't ready for that and that he wouldn't try it again, and he didn't. He just held me mostly."

Morgan shook her head as if in disbelief. "Guys like him aren't typically very patient. He must have it bad for you." She smirked. "What kind of magic vagina are *you* hiding down there?"

"Shut up!" I laughed again and stuck my freezing fingers to the vent, where heat poured out.

"You know, it's okay for you to move on to someone else, Juliet," Morgan said softly.

"Maybe one day," I answered vaguely.

She didn't reply, so I knew she didn't agree. She wanted me to be over Drake already so I could move on with my life. Though I appreciated that she wanted better for me than to be stuck in a rapid cycle of grief, I knew that healing would happen in its own time. I couldn't rush it or push myself.

We parked in front of my apartment building, and I reached across the console to give her a quick hug before getting out of the car. I waved as I watched her drive away and started climbing the stairs to my front door. I let myself in and slipped my heels off by the door and headed to the kitchen to pour myself a glass of red wine. I took it to the living room and sank onto the couch, my feet up underneath me.

I needed to get a cat. Something to make me feel a little less lonely when I was here by myself, and let's face it, I was always here by myself. Aside from the weekend movie fests Morgan and I sometimes had, Hayden coming in that night from the bar was the first time I'd had another person in my apartment since I'd moved in a year and a half ago. The first time a man had stepped foot in my apartment other than the maintenance guy. It had felt natural that he was in my space, and I think that's what scared me the most.

If someone took one glance at Hayden, they'd think he was no good. I'd taken that impression to heart when I'd first met him, and I felt badly about it. He'd proven to me he was actually a very decent man. He'd taken me home drunk and hadn't laid a finger on me other than to gently move me away, and he'd backed off when I'd panicked over the kiss he'd tried to give me. Not many men would do that. Most would make the best of the situation and try to get in my pants, trying to get me to do things I wasn't ready for. That made me want to give him an honest chance, though I had no idea what he was even searching for. He hadn't said if he wanted a fling or if he was wanting something more serious. I was leaning toward the former. He had to go back home to

London at some point, and I thought I was done with long-distance relationships for the remainder of my life.

Could I do it, though? Could I really let myself get involved with someone who would just be walking away from me at the end? I sat there contemplating it, mulling over how I'd feel if I gave myself to him knowing there was a definite end. I needed to find out how long he was going to be here. That was the only way to determine if I could go through with it.

I let my gaze drift across the couch to the side table. My picture of Drake that I'd gotten framed after his death sat there propped up on its kickstand.

"Is it time for me to move on from you, sweetheart?" I asked, but there was obviously no answer. I was talking to a dead man, someone I'd never hear laugh or see smile again. Tears blurred my vision, and I didn't hold them back.

Curling into the couch I let myself go, allowing the pain swallow me up for the moment. I was sobbing into the back of my couch when my phone rang. Not a message, but a call. Without checking to see who it was, I answered.

"Hello?" My voice was thick with tears and scratchy from crying.

"Juliet? Are you okay?"

"Hayden? Yeah, uh, I'm fine. I'm okay. Hard day at work," I lied.

"Do you need me to bring you anything?"

Was there no end to his kindness? I almost felt like I didn't deserve it.

"No, I'll be fine. I'm just drowning myself in wine and trying to prepare for tomorrow."

"Let me know if you change your mind. I was actually calling to see if you were free on Friday evening. We settled on bowling then, and I'd still like for you to come if you can."

He still wanted to see me, even after I'd gotten weird about him trying to kiss me. Maybe Morgan was right and he did want more than just sex from me. But why? If he was just going to be leaving to go back home, why would he care about building up a relationship with me?

"Sure, I don't have anything planned for then."

He exhaled, as if he were relieved. "Excellent. I'll pick you up at seven."

"Seven it is." A moment of silence passed between us before I spoke again. "Hayden?"

"Yeah?"

"Thank you for being a decent guy. It's just — I'm just having a hard time getting over some things. I don't want you to think I don't like you. I do, I really do. I just need some time, and I know time isn't really on our side since you'll have to go back home eventually. So I'd understand if you wanted to give up on me." I was giving him an out, even though it pained me to do so.

"Give up? And why would I do that?"

I stammered, "Well, I, um, I don't know. It's just, there have to be other women out there who can give you what you want without any hang-ups like I have. You're an attractive man, it shouldn't be too hard for you to find, uh, to get . . ." I trailed off.

"Sex? If that's all I wanted then I would have gotten it already, love."

I bit my lip as I thought it over. So he didn't just want me for sex? "What do you want from me?" I whispered into the phone.

His accent thickened, and his voice came out like smooth velvet when he said, "I want you, sure, I won't deny it, but I want more than that, too. I want to know you and know that when you think of what makes you happy, my face comes to mind. If you need time to get there, then I'll give it to you.

Don't worry about when I go back home. We'll deal with that when the time comes."

"Okay," I said, not knowing what else to say. He wanted my trust and he wanted me to think of him in terms of happiness. Those were both a very big deal for me and they would only come with time. I didn't know if he even had the patience for how long it would take. Or the time.

Voices called out his name on the other end of the line, and he sighed. "I've got to go now, but I'll see you on Friday, okay?"

"Friday," I confirmed.

"Goodnight, Juliet."

"Night, Hayden." When the line went dead, I stared at my phone, and a slow smile spread. I had another date, only this time it would be with him and his friends. I had to make an impression, and that started with my outfit. If they were anything like Hayden, then I figured they'd be rough bikers or something of the sort. What did one wear to meet bikers?

I took my wineglass with me to the bedroom and riffled through my closet. I didn't own anything edgy or cool. It was mostly a closet full of professional attire for work, blouses, and sweaters. I pulled out a dark-gray cashmere sweater and a pair of skinny jeans with little rips and tears in the legs that I'd let Morgan convince me to buy last time we'd gone shopping. I hadn't had a chance to wear them yet, but now seemed like a good time to break them in.

Scanning through my shoes, I settled on my favorite pair of sparkly black flats. My feet would probably get cold, but I liked the way they paired with the sweater so decided to make the sacrifice.

With my outfit picked out, I threw myself onto the bed and turned on the bedroom TV. I felt a little lighter than I had before knowing I'd be seeing Hayden again in a few days. When I was with him, I could almost forget about the dark cloud that seemed to follow me everywhere I went these last few months. I couldn't completely forget, though. I felt the shame that came with moving on. Drake would never laugh again, never tell me he loved me, never send me another sweet message, and here I was going on dates and thinking of another man.

What would Drake want me to do, though? Surely he wouldn't want me to wallow in depression over his death forever. He'd want me to be happy, like Morgan had said over and over again. Drake had been such a good, gracious man. I'd never known anyone like that in all my years. I think that's what had drawn me to him in the first place. If he were peering down at me now, I'd like to think he'd be happy knowing I was getting out of the house again and socializing with someone other than just Morgan. That piece of me that wasn't totally broken by the loss wanted to believe he *would* be happy for me.

I sighed and downed the rest of my wine. There was no way to know how Drake would feel because he wasn't around to tell me. We'd never talked morbidly about what would happen should one of us pass on. I hadn't even known he'd put me down as his top emergency contact until the hospital had called to tell me he had died, though I knew he didn't have anybody else important in his life. His parents were both gone, and he'd had an estranged brother, but that was it.

Focusing on the TV, I flipped through channels until I found a movie. I used to watch these really cheesy romance movies with one of my foster parents growing up. She was a single older woman, but she'd dreamed of love more than any teenager I'd ever met. We'd sit down in front of the TV with a made-for-TV movie, and she'd sigh longingly when the heroine of the story finally kissed the hero. She'd smile at me and say, "One day we're both going to have that."

I hadn't believed her much. I hadn't believed in love. Not until I'd met Drake. That had changed everything for me. Miss Caroline was probably the only foster parent I had that I actually liked, though. The only reason I couldn't continue staying with her was because her dad got sick and she had to move out of state and therefore had to give me up.

I remembered her crying when they came to take me away. She hugged me tightly, apologizing as she'd kissed my face. "One day, something good is going to happen to you, Juliet. I can feel it," she'd said.

I hadn't let myself cry until I was lying in bed back at the children's home that night.

I still talked to her on occasion. We called each other for updates, and last I heard she was living in Fresno, engaged to a widower who had four kids. I knew she'd always wanted kids, so I was happy for her. She was one of the few people in my life who understood my hang-up on Drake. I think a lot of it had to do with her hopeless romantic trait, but it still felt nice knowing someone out there got it.

I checked the clock on my bedside table—nine o'clock. It would still be early in California, so I picked up my phone and dialed her number.

"Juliet Banks, it's been too long," she chirped into the phone.

I immediately smiled. Her enthusiasm was contagious. "Yes, it has. I have a lot to tell you." I told her all about Hayden, right down to the very last detail of our night out at the Wayward Druid. When I finished, she sighed dreamily.

"It sounds like you've got the makings of a good love story there, my dear," she said with a smile in her voice.

"I feel guilty, though, and I can't seem to move past it."

"Because of Drake?"

She got me. I should have called her a long time ago.

"Yes. It feels wrong to forget about him and move on."

"Oh, sweetie, you'll never forget about him. Moving on doesn't mean forgetting. It just means that you aren't living stuck in the past. I never did get the chance to speak with him, but if Drake was half the man you'd told me he was, he would be ecstatic that you've found someone. We don't get many chances to love in this life, Juliet. When we find it, we have to hold on with both hands and ride it out."

Tears pricked my eyes. It was by far the best advice I'd been given, and it lessened the pain.

"Thank you, Miss Caroline. I wouldn't go as far as to say this is love, though. We just barely know each other."

"For now," she said without missing a beat. "You'll get to know this Hayden better, and I hope you like what you discover. I have to say, the motorcycle makes me a little nervous, but I guess that's just the mother in me." She laughed.

"It makes me nervous, too," I admitted, "but it wasn't as bad as I thought it'd be." It had been the single freest moment of my life, and I longed to feel the wind blow past me again, though I wouldn't tell her that. I was Juliet Banks. I didn't take risks like hopping on motorcycles with a dashing and albeit mysterious man.

"Just take care of yourself, sweetie, and remember what I said. You deserve some happiness after all that life has thrown your way."

I thanked her for the advice, and we ended the call. I laid my phone on my bedside table and focused in on the TV. The movie was still on, at least halfway through. I had no idea what was going on, but the heroine of the story was struggling with her feelings for the hero. I could empathize.

It was too early for me to have any feelings of real substance for Hayden, but I couldn't deny that I felt *something* there. Whether it was extreme like or lust, I didn't know, but I thought that maybe it was extreme like. Sure, he had the body of a god and the face of an angel, but I liked him as a person, too. I liked everything I was slowly finding out about him, except the gambling and fighting. Those things I could do without.

But I also knew I couldn't change him. If the poker and fighting were a part of him, could I just accept that and move past it? I didn't really know. I didn't fully know what I wanted from him. He'd told me he wanted more than sex from me, but I didn't know if that's what *I* wanted.

I sighed and closed my eyes. I still had about three days to figure some things out. I'd take that time to really evaluate the situation and decide what I wanted. Hayden wasn't pressing me to make any decisions about him. All the pressure was coming from me and me alone. In fact, he'd been nothing short of patient and understanding that I was having some hang-ups about moving forward.

The rest of the night, I tried not to think about it as I watched movie after movie of unsuspecting couples finding love in places they'd least expected it. I might have even cried a few times when the guy made grand gestures of love to win over the girl. I felt like everyone deserved love like that. I'd had it and lost it, but maybe, just maybe, it was possible that I would one day find it again.

Chapter Seven

The next few days passed without much word from Hayden. It was like he sensed I needed space to think and had given that to me. The only problem was it was now Friday afternoon, and I was still no closer to making a decision than I'd been on Tuesday.

I racked my brain to the point of headache trying to find a way past my feelings of guilt and remorse for even thinking of leaving Drake behind. I was just stuck. Stuck in my feelings and unable to move past them. Morgan even tried talking me through my thought process, and although I could see how irrational I was being, it didn't change much.

So I sat at my desk cleaning up files on my computer as I waited for five o'clock to roll around. The hairs on the back of my neck stood up, and I turned, knowing Carter was standing there. Even my body had an uncanny sixth sense when it came to him. I was repulsed by even the thought of him being near me.

"Juliet, how's your day going?" he asked leaning against my cubicle wall.

"Just fine, sir," I answered, glancing at the clock behind him. Four forty-two. Almost time to go.

"I was wondering if you'd stay late tonight to work on an extra file."

"I'm sorry, I have plans, otherwise I would. I promise I'll catch the next one?"

His mouth thinned out, but he nodded. "What plans do you have?"

The question took me by surprise. Normally he just took my words at face value and left me alone. I didn't much like him digging into my personal life.

"Oh, just going out with some friends. Nothing big."

Carter smiled and excused himself, slipping away to find some other poor soul to stay behind after work. I wouldn't have wanted to stay even if I had nothing to do but go home and sleep, though I could have used the extra money. I still had plenty of student loans to pay back. It was only a reminder of how royally I'd screwed myself.

I watched the clock tick away to five o'clock and hurried to grab up my things and leave before someone could stop me. In the garage I waited impatiently for Morgan to arrive to take me home. My car was still being a pain, and I knew it was time to bite the bullet and have it looked at. Maybe I could take it to Berkley's place. After all, he was the only mechanic I knew personally by name. But my car did this every now and then before leveling back out and running like a dream all over again.

"Let's go out for drinks tonight. I'm feeling extra shitty today," Morgan called out when she drew nearer.

"Oh, I'm actually going out with Hayden tonight. I'll cancel, and you can tell me all about your day." I found my phone, but she snatched it from me.

"Don't you dare cancel. We can go out tomorrow night."

"But what kind of friend would I be if I left you hanging when you needed me?" I did want to see Hayden but I was a little nervous about meeting any more of his friends. Berkley had been nice, more than nice, but I didn't know that they all would be.

"You're my best friend, and I appreciate you wanting to give up a night out with perfection incarnate to be with me, but I would never forgive myself if I let you do this. You're dating again, Juliet, and you deserve it after everything. Just go and have fun, for me if for nothing else." She gave me a tight hug and laid a kiss on my cheek. "Let's get you home so you can get ready."

Morgan followed me upstairs to go over my wardrobe choice and makeup. To my surprise, she didn't argue over my outfit. She claimed it was classy but sexy. I didn't tell her, but that was exactly what I'd been going for.

She helped me brush on my makeup. Silvery-gray eyeshadow with a smoky black smudge of eyeliner, mascara, and a deep red lipstick. I looked a lot more badass than I felt. When she left it was nearly seven, so I poured myself a glass of wine for courage.

I was just rinsing the glass out when Hayden knocked on my door. Though I wanted to rush over and throw the door open, I made myself take a second for composure and then crossed the small distance between the kitchen and front door. When I opened it, he stood there in a dark-blue shirt under his leather jacket, jeans, and those same worn-in boots. He smiled, his dimples making their appearance, and I found myself smiling back.

"You're beautiful," he said, raking his gaze over my face and body. His gaze was searing, and primal desire clouded his eyes. He licked his lips and continued his slow assessment.

My face flamed hotly, and I muttered, "Thank you."

"Let's get out of here before I change my mind about going anywhere," he said with a rough edge to his voice.

A shiver ripped through me while I pictured him slowly peeling my clothes from my body and fucking me on my living room floor.

He took my hand, his palm burning against mine, and we went down the stairs, crossing the parking lot to his motorcycle. I wasn't quite as apprehensive about climbing onto it this time as I was before. I was almost giddy. He passed me the helmet, and I pushed it down onto my head. He put his own on and climbed on. I swung my leg over the back and settled in behind him, ready for that sweet scent of mint to cascade over me. It hit me, and I sighed, snuggling in closer. He stiffened just a fraction of a second before he relaxed and patted my hands that were wrapped tightly around him.

Using his foot to put up the kickstand, Hayden started the motorcycle's engine, and we peeled away. There was only one bowling alley that I knew of in town—Star Lanes, on Belcher Street just off the main highway next to the movie theater. I noticed that's where we were heading, and I felt a little relieved. I guess I had this image of him taking me into the bad part of town to hang out at a run-down bowling alley with his rowdy friends. I still wasn't sure about the friends, but I at least knew we were going to be in a well-lit part of town.

We stopped in a parking spot in the lot. I released my death grip on him and removed the helmet. I hopped down off the bike and caught him smiling at me.

"What?"

"You like riding my bike, don't you?"

The question caught me off guard, so when I didn't answer, he stepped closer and looked me in the eye.

"You like that it's a little dangerous, because you've never done a dangerous thing in your life. Your cheeks are red, and your eyes are bright with excitement. If I'd known that's what it took to make you happy, I would have been taking you on rides every day."

"I guess I do kind of like it," I admitted.

His smile grew wider, and he wrapped me up in his arms, hugging me close.

"Come on, daredevil, let's go inside. I think everyone is already here."

The nerves hit me again. I remembered we were meeting

his friends here. How did someone from London have more than one friend in America already after a month of being here? I had to imagine he didn't come by them by normal means.

He held the door open for me, and I walked in, the smell of stale sweat and leather shoes permeating the air.

"Hayden, good to see you. Berkley and the others are on lanes two and three," the man behind the counter said, jerking his thumb over his shoulder.

I was glad to know Berkley was here. I'd have at least one person to talk to other than Hayden if the rest of his friends ended up not liking me.

We switched out our shoes for bowling shoes—I'd brought socks along since I'd been wearing my flats—and made our way over to the lanes where Hayden's friends gathered. I half hid behind him, and he said his greetings, but he led me up next to him by my hand and tucked me into his side.

"Guys, this is Juliet. Juliet, this is Garrett." He pointed to a guy taller than even he was with a muscular body and an eyebrow ring. His hair was blond, and he had dull blue eyes. He smiled at me and nodded a greeting. "Adam." He gestured to a short, stocky man with close-cropped brown hair and the lightest brown eyes. He had a single gold hoop in his ear and he also gave me a warm smile. "And Jade."

I turned to Hayden's left, where a leggy thin woman stood with her arms crossed over her ample chest. She was eyeing me up and down. Her eyes were the most striking shade of blue I'd ever seen, lined in dark kohl. Even in the chill of February she was wearing a t-shirt with the sleeves cut off, exposing arms covered in tattoos from fingertips to shoulder. Streaks of cobalt blue were highlighted throughout the blonde in her hair.

I definitely felt out of place in this group of people. They were all dressed in band tees and worn-in jeans while I was dressed almost as if I were going to a casual office party.

"And the little thing already knows me," Berkley interjected with a wink.

"Pleasure as always, Berkley," I smiled.

"Welcome to the party." Garrett smiled wider, watching Hayden and me mischievously.

Hayden leaned down and told me he was going to grab us some drinks and he'd be right back. I nodded and watched him walk away.

"You aren't really his type, so what gives?"

I jerked my gaze away from Hayden to find Jade standing right in front of me, glowering.

"Excuse me?" I wasn't sure I'd heard her correctly, but her tone suggested she didn't like me one bit.

"You aren't what he usually goes for. You do realize he's probably using you, right?"

The thought had crossed my mind that I wasn't what he normally gravitated toward and I'd even questioned his motives many times over the past week thanks to it. Regardless, I didn't like this girl voicing my greatest fear in this thing out loud.

"Do you have a problem with me?" I asked, bunching my eyebrows together.

"Hayden and I have a . . . history. Trust me when I say he's only going to crush you." She sounded bitter and as jaded as her name suggested.

I was hoping for some backup, but the other three guys were too busy crowding around the computer putting in nicknames for one another, and Hayden was still at the counter.

"I'll take my chances, thanks," I replied softly. I didn't do well with confrontation, and Jade seemed like someone who thrived on it.

"Don't say I didn't warn you. And don't come crying to me when it inevitably happens." She tossed her colored hair over her shoulder, sneered at me, and moved over to the computer with the guys.

I was left standing there like an idiot.

My face must have given me away, because Hayden returned then and frowned. "What's wrong?"

"Not a thing." I tried wiping the baffled and guarded expression from my face. I didn't want to believe Jade was right, but she'd said they had a history, and that could only mean one thing. They'd been together at some point, and it hadn't ended well. I couldn't very well expect any better than that when she seemed every bit his type and I just didn't.

"Are you sure?" He glanced between Jade and me.

He'd obviously seen us talking, but I wasn't going to rat her out for being hostile toward me. Jade was his friend, and I was simply someone he barely knew. I wasn't going to cause trouble where there wasn't any.

"Positive," I answered, smiling up at him.

He passed me the cold glass of beer he'd brought for me, and I gulped down a sip. I wasn't usually a beer type of girl, but that was about all they served at the bowling alley other than sodas, and I was definitely going to need some form of alcohol to get through tonight.

"Hayden, you're up first," Berkley called over his shoulder.

Hayden looked at me one last time, then set his beer down and grabbed a ball, but I knew this conversation was far from over.

He skidded to a stop right before the lane and released the ball. It expertly rolled down the length of floor, knocking over all but one pin.

"So close," Adam mocked with a laugh.

"Fuck you, let's see you do better," Hayden challenged him after rolling the ball again, laying down the last pin.

"Lucky for us, my turn is up." Adam brought the ball up, swung it back, then rolled it hard down the lane. He also knocked down every pin but one.

"Just as I thought," Hayden said smugly, clapping Adam on the back.

"Yeah, yeah," Adam muttered and lined up his second shot, only to miss.

"You two aren't going to have a dick measuring contest all night, are you?" Jade asked. "I've seen them both and I think we all know who's is bigger." She cut her gaze to me, almost gloating.

Hayden's eyes hardened as he gave her a warning glare. My cheeks grew hot, from embarrassment or anger, I didn't know, but I did know I didn't like how Jade was acting toward me. I'd done nothing to her, but she was certainly taking my being there as a threat.

"You're up, love," Hayden called to me, pulling me out of my head.

"I have to admit, I haven't been bowling since I was a child. So don't laugh too hard if it goes right in the gutter." I was going to make an idiot of myself and I knew it. Typically, I could have laughed it off, but Jade made me uncomfortable, and I didn't want to give her more of a reason to see me as Hayden's pathetic playmate.

"Here, I'll help you."

I grabbed a neon pink ball, and Hayden stepped up behind me to show me how to position myself. With his hands on my hips, he adjusted my stance, and when his fingers came over mine to show me the correct way to hold the ball, my breathing shallowed. Just a simple touch from him was enough for my whole system to go haywire.

"And when you feel comfortable, draw back and release."

I focused on the pins at the end of the lane, positioned myself the way Hayden had shown me, then rolled the ball as hard as I could. I watched through my fingers as it continued on down the lane without falling into the gutter. It hit one pin, which set off a chain reaction until every pin was down. I'd gotten a strike.

"Not bad for someone who hasn't played in years," Berkley complimented me. "If we were betting on the game I'd say you were conning us."

"Who, me?" I placed my hands over my heart and pulled a mock shocked face. "I would never."

"Yeah, you seem innocent, but I'm willing to bet you're ruthless when it comes down to it," Garrett joked.

"I guess you'll just have to wait and see," I quipped, walking over to Hayden, who wrapped his arm around my waist and dragged me into his side. He smirked down at me, only one little dimple surfacing. I didn't think I would ever tire of watching those dimples pockmark his cheeks. They softened his hard edges, made him appear younger, though I didn't actually have a clue how old he was.

"Hey, how old are you?" I asked him.

"Thirty-two," he answered. That made him seven years older than me. "That doesn't bother you, does it?"

"Nope," I assured him.

His face relaxed. He'd been worried, I realized, that it would be a deal breaker for me. It's true that he was the oldest guy I'd involved myself with, but he was hardly old at thirty-two. And besides, I still didn't even know what this was. I was enjoying his company, and it was a welcome distraction from that thundercloud that was hovering over my head, but I still wasn't sure if I was ready for anything more. Though Miss Caroline and Morgan had given me sound advice and told me that it wouldn't be a bad thing to give Hayden an honest chance, now I couldn't get Jade's words out of my mind. I needed to be careful around Hayden. I had to protect my heart from being broken again.

By the end of the game Hayden and Adam were tied, Garrett came in second, Jade came in third, Berkley was fourth, and I came in dead last. Regardless of the severe loss, I'd had fun. I'd just pretended Jade wasn't there for the better part of the night, though she shot me dirty glares every time Hayden touched me or leaned down to say something in my ear.

"It was nice meeting you, Juliet," Garrett said, yanking me into a bear hug. Berkley followed with his own hug, and Adam patted me on the head. Jade side-eyed me and said nothing, though she didn't need to. Her face said everything. *You're encroaching on my territory. Watch your back.*

We all got our shoes back and made our way out to the motorcycle.

"Are you hungry?" Hayden asked me then. "I'm starving."

"I could eat," I replied with a nod.

"I know the perfect place." He smiled as he pushed his helmet down over his head and we zoomed from the parking lot.

Chapter Eight

Hayden rolled the bike into the parking lot of a little diner called Rosa's. I had never been there before. It truthfully wasn't somewhere I would have ever thought to go. I could just imagine the clogged arteries the greasy food would produce, but after drinking on an empty stomach, I'd eat just about anything.

It was nice and warm inside, and we settled into a booth across from each other. I picked up the menu, which showed typical diner food. Burgers, sandwiches, hot dogs. I settled on getting just a standard cheeseburger with a side of homemade fries.

"Welcome to Rosa's. What can I get you kids to drink?" Our waitress was a plump older woman with bottle-dyed blonde hair, and she sounded like she smoked two packs a day. Her nametag read Starla.

"Diet cola," I answered.

"I'll have the same," Hayden said, smiling at her.

"I'll grab your drinks and be back for your dinner order." She ambled off, limping slightly on her left leg.

I could feel Hayden's eyes on me, so I focused harder on the menu, though I already knew what I wanted. He reached across the table and took my hand in his. The contact sizzled my skin and crackled with electric vibrations.

"Juliet," he began, but Starla had returned with our drinks.

I jerked my hand away and grabbed my drink to take a sip. Starla took our orders and disappeared again.

"What did Jade say to you?" He got right to the point, no screwing around.

If it weren't for the subject matter making me uncomfortable, I might appreciate that he didn't tiptoe around things.

"Nothing," I said, not meeting his eyes.

"Look at me."

I let my eyes find his.

His black eyes were soft and probing. "I know she said something. I saw you two talking, and you seemed uncomfortable for the rest of the night."

I sighed and decided honesty was the best policy. I didn't particularly want to cause any issues between the two friends, but he wasn't going to drop it, and I knew it. "She said you two had a history and that you were going to break my heart. And then that comment about her seeing your . . . well, you know."

His face gave nothing away, but he cursed under his breath. "Jade and I, we kissed. One time. But that's it, I promise. There isn't as much history there as she led you to believe. We were both drunk after one of Berkley's band's concerts, and she came on to me. She kissed me, and I didn't push her away. Things have been a little different between us since then. She's tried to get me alone on more than one occasion, but I've tried making it clear we're just friends. The lead singer of the band is her older brother, and even if I was inclined to have anything to do with her in that way, and I'm not, he'd kick my ass. And about seeing my dick, she walked in on me changing at Berkley's last week. I never fucked her."

I just stared at him, trying to find a hint of deception, but all I saw was truth. I wanted to believe him. I wasn't sure I could continue hanging around Jade if I knew she and Hayden had slept together. It would be far too awkward for me.

"As for the other thing," he said, running a hand through

his jet-black hair, "I don't know where this is going to go, but I'd like to see where it takes us. I don't want to hurt you, and I think if you'd give it a chance, you'd see that I mean that wholly."

"Okay, thank you for clearing that up," I replied, not sure what else to say. He wanted me to take a chance on him, but I was scared out of my mind. Even if there'd been no truth to what Jade had said, I couldn't shake the feeling that maybe it wasn't too far off the mark. If I put my faith in him and what we could have together, I was giving him the power to utterly destroy me. What if I got attached and he ended up going back to London? I wasn't sure I'd be able to handle essentially losing two men within a few months of each other. "I need time to think," I finally said.

He nodded and took my hand again, stroking the side with his thumb. "I can work with that. But I'll tell you, love, though I'm a patient man, I'm not a blind one. I know if I don't snatch you up someone else will try to, and for that reason, I'm not going to give up."

Warmth bloomed in my chest and fanned out at his spoken confession. I said a silent prayer to Drake that he would hopefully forgive me for even entertaining this thing with Hayden. On the off chance that Miss Caroline and Morgan were right, I didn't want to just let life slip past me like I had these last few months. Not when I had a man standing in front of me telling me he wasn't going to give up on me.

So I wasn't quite ready for the physical aspect of a relationship. I could get used to the rest, and that would follow naturally. Not to mention it had been over three years since my last partner. I was almost afraid I'd forgotten how sex worked. There was no telling at this point if I'd be a good partner.

"Here you go, hon." Starla returned with two plates and set them in front of us.

I immediately took a bite so I wouldn't have to answer Hayden. Even with me harboring the burden of grief, perched on my shoulders like a bird of prey, I didn't want Hayden to give up. It was selfish of me to expect him to keep coming around when I couldn't even get out of my own head enough to kiss him, but I liked knowing that someone considered me worth fighting for. I barely knew this guy, but I found myself *wanting* to know him. I liked his lines and edges, but I sensed something softer in him, and I liked that, too. Hayden was by far the most intriguing man I'd ever met, and something about that called to me, beckoned me to dive farther in and discover who he was on the inside.

We ate and talked about the bowling game, Hayden bragging about his superior skills while I made self-depreciating jokes about mine. All talk of Jade had disappeared, much to my relief, and things seemed to migrate into comfortable banter. I loosened up more as we sat there long after finishing our meal, just talking.

"What's your biggest dream?" he asked me then.

I didn't even have to think twice about it. "My parents always had this dream of owning a bed and breakfast here in the village past town. They talked about it constantly, building off one another's ideas. The older I got, the more I wanted to open one myself in their honor. I came pretty close last year, but the place I'd chosen had been bought out by someone else, and I was back to square one. There isn't a day that goes by that I don't remember how much the idea meant to them, so it means a lot to me, too. So I guess my biggest dream would be to carry out their dream for them."

"Good answer," he said softly with the touch of a smile.

"What about you?"

"I guess my biggest dream currently would be to get to know you better." He smirked.

I rolled my eyes and tossed a napkin at him. "I'm being

serious," I pointed out.

"So am I."

We locked gazes and said nothing for a long moment.

"I guess I should get you home," he said.

A twinge of sadness rose in me that the night was coming to an end, but I still stood and followed him from the diner into the biting cold. The entire ride home I hugged myself to his back and listened to his breathing. It was steady and calm, the opposite of how I was currently feeling. Being near him, touching him, sent my body on a whirlwind roller coaster of emotions. I felt giddy, I felt desire, I felt guilt. But most of all, I felt like it was right, perfect. I'd never felt that way when touching someone before. I would have liked to think I'd have felt that way with Drake, but I'd never know now. All I had to go on were my current feelings regarding Hayden.

We rolled into a spot in front of my building and walked the two flights up to my apartment door. I sucked in a breath preparing to ask something that could shift the tides of our relationship.

"Do you want to come in and watch a movie with me? I'm not really tired, and I don't really want to be alone, either. And if I know Morgan, she's definitely busy." She probably had her thighs wrapped around some guy's head about right now. I tried to ignore the stab of jealousy I felt knowing she could easily hop into bed with someone while I was struggling to make it to first base.

"I'd love to, but I'm picking the movie."

"Nothing boring, please," I begged him.

He smiled wickedly, and I let us into the apartment.

"I think the guide is already on if you turn the TV on. I'll go make some popcorn." I went to the kitchen and found a bag of popcorn, shoved it into the microwave, and hit the appropriate button. When it beeped to let me know it was done, I got it out and dumped the whole thing into an over-sized bowl. I carried it and two colas into the living room and plopped down on the couch next to Hayden. I expected it to be weird that he was here in my space while I was totally sober, but it felt kind of nice. Like it was something we'd done a thousand times.

"How do you feel about horror movies?" he asked, scrolling through the list of movies.

"I don't mind them, but I'll probably hide my eyes the whole time," I answered honestly.

He settled on a title named *The Haunting of Brimley Oaks*. The synopsis said it was about a haunted house, and the story it told was of the last family who'd lived there. It was apparently a true story, not that I put much faith in it. I didn't really believe in ghosts and the like.

I grabbed a handful of popcorn and settled back into the couch. Hayden threw a piece into the air and caught it with his mouth. I laughed and tried to do the same, but it only hit my nose and bounced off.

"It takes major skill," he explained to me, demonstrating again how it was done.

I found my gaze lingering on his plump lips, wondering what they'd taste like. I glanced away, back to the TV, when his arm came around me. I snuggled deeper into him and laid my head on his shoulder.

The opening of the movie showed a young family of four moving their things into their new home that honestly seemed like it should have been condemned a century ago. It was a large Victorian with lots of wrought iron. So far everything was still happy and peaceful.

Hayden's fingers threaded and sifted through my hair, lulling me into a feeling of divine comfort. It felt good being here in his arms, even for something as innocent as watching a movie together.

"I bet you one of the kids sees something and the adults don't believe them until it's too late," he said. "That's how it always goes."

"Either that, or one of the kids ends up going missing or they get hurt and the adults try to rationalize it until they come face to face with the ghost themselves. But again, by then it's too late."

We shared a laugh because these movies were so typically transparent, even if the jump-out-at-you scenes always got me.

Thirty minutes later I was glued to the screen. The oldest kid was creeping through the house at night with a flashlight. He'd heard footsteps outside his door, so he obviously had to investigate. Suddenly, his flashlight cut out, plunging him into darkness. I threw my hands up over my face and peeked through my fingers. The character banged the light on his palm, and when it cut back on, a ghost was standing there right in front of him. I screamed and jumped, the popcorn bowl in my lap turning over onto the floor. Luckily it was half gone, so I had less to clean up.

Hayden roared with laughter, throwing his head back.

"It's not funny," I protested, slapping his chest.

He caught my hand and laced his fingers through mine.

"It's a little funny, love."

I pouted and got down on the floor to pick up the bits of popcorn.

When I finished, I stuck the bowl on the coffee table and knelt. I was directly between Hayden's legs. He peered down at me, carnal desire open and apparent in his fathomless eyes. I blushed what had to be a brilliant red and scrambled back onto the couch next to him. I wasn't sure what had come over me, but in that moment I'd wanted to throw myself in his arms and kiss him. Maybe it was just the frustration of being sexless for years and having him here now, or maybe it was the way he'd been staring down at me. My breathing had shallowed, and my chest rose and fell rapidly while my heart banged against my ribcage. I spared a glance at Hayden to see that he was also having trouble breathing. Then I glanced down. The unmistakable outline of his hard-on curved the seam of his jeans. I bit down on my bottom lip and turned to face him.

"Hayden?"

"Yes, love?" His voice had grown huskier, deeper.

"If I told you to kiss me right now, would you?"

He turned to me then, his eyes alight with the flame of longing. "You're damn right I would. Just say the word."

I thought it over a moment. What could one little kiss hurt? It had been so long since I'd been close to someone physically, and it ached to be so near Hayden without doing anything about it. I scooted closer to him and placed my hand on his chest.

"Kiss me," I begged softly.

He moved closer, his head dipping down. He brushed his lips along the corner of my mouth so tenderly, then took my mouth with his. The kiss was sensual and languorous, un-hurried. His tongue lapped at my lips, and I opened my mouth to give him access. His tongue immediately darted in and danced with mine. A strong tingle started between my thighs and worked its way throughout my whole body as I shook under his kiss.

He pushed me down onto the couch, hovering over me and kissing me deeply. I dug my hands into his hair, pulling him down harder on my mouth. I wanted more, so much more. All the same, he never relented his slow, tantalizing pace, and his mouth released mine only to pepper gentle kisses against my jaw. He drifted down farther to rake his tongue across my neck, and a strangled moan escaped me, while he grunted. His hips were digging into mine, his growing desire right up against me, right where I wanted him to touch me.

He whispered into my ear in a hoarse voice, "Do you have any idea what you do to me, Juliet?"

Those words, so familiar. They were words Drake had murmured to me over the phone right after we'd had incredibly hot phone sex. Those words coupled with his similar accent made me stiffen.

Hayden sat back and looked down at me with concern. "Did I say something wrong?" he asked, running a hand through his tousled hair.

"N-no. No, it isn't you. It's me. I'm . . . I think I'm broken." Tears filled my eyes quickly. I tried blinking them away, but that only resulted in sending them spilling over onto my cheeks.

Hayden gathered me up into his arms and muttered soothing words to me as he held me tightly. "What makes you think you're broken?"

I had vaguely told him about Drake's car accident, but I hadn't told him how badly it affected me. But I felt now was a good time to have that hard conversation. Hayden needed to know what he was getting himself into. I'd tell him everything, and I'd give him the chance to walk away from me now.

Drawing in a breath, I began. "I told you about my boyfriend dying in a car accident months ago. But I didn't explain everything."

I paused, and he watched me, expression guarded while I continued.

"He was planning on coming here three days after the accident occurred, but he was dead before it could happen. It would have been our first time meeting in person. We'd been together for a year, and I really, truly loved him. He was everything I thought I wanted in another person. And now, I find myself very attracted to you, but I can't get rid of this overwhelming guilt I feel. He hasn't been gone all that long, and here I am asking another man to kiss me and fantasizing about other things that I used to only dream of him doing to me. I feel like I'm betraying him somehow by moving on with my life as if he never existed." I choked up, a sob breaking through my words. Still, I powered on. "I like you a lot, Hayden, and I'm trying so hard not to continue letting my past relationship with a dead man prevent me from living my life, but I see him everywhere.

"Everyone keeps telling me that he'd want me to live my life and find someone else to make me happy, and I know they're right. Drake was the most selfless person I'd ever known. And if the tables were reversed, I know I'd want him to move on and be happy. Pining over someone who isn't around anymore isn't healthy." I paused to catch my breath and finally turned to Hayden, who seemed almost tortured. "I guess what I'm trying to say is this—I want you, very much. I've never been so aware of my own body as I am when I'm around you. I think about you all the time, and I think about what it would be like being with you in bed. But I can't seem to get past this horrid grip his death has on me, and I don't know what to do about it."

Hayden was so quiet I was almost afraid he wouldn't say anything at all. He scrubbed his hand down his face and blinked a few times before turning back to me. "I'm really sorry you're having such a hard time with it, love. I wish I knew how to help you through it, but I've never dealt well with loss myself, and I've lost a lot of people. Never someone I was in love with, but people I did care deeply about. I'm not going to push you to get over him, if that's what you're afraid of. That has to come in its own time. But I do want to be in your life and I am going to fight like hell to keep you around."

"But, why? As Jade so aptly pointed out tonight, I'm not exactly your type, and for lack of a better description, I'm kind of fucked up."

He smiled sadly and brushed a tear from my cheek. "We're all a little fucked up, aren't we? And I wouldn't put much faith in anything Jade says. She wants to scare you away from me, and I truly hope she doesn't. I like you a lot, Juliet. I did from the moment I saw you. I'm not going to just walk away because you're dealing with some shit. What kind of person would that make me?"

A smart person in my opinion. I did have to admit, though, it felt good to get some of the oppressing weight off my chest. It was like the more I talked about it, the easier it was to live with.

"Tell me more about Drake."

"He was really kind, that more than anything. He worked as an accountant at this very successful firm in London and he was probably the most stable boyfriend I'd ever had. I went through a period of really horrible choices. We talked constantly, messages, calls sometimes, video chats. We even sent each other letters occasionally. He was so romantic and always talked about our future together. For the first time in a relationship, I saw things heading in a bright direction. I had something nice to look forward to." I smiled to myself as I remembered the many late-night conversations we'd had where Drake had gone on about how great our life could be together. It had all been so perfect. "He was every-thing good in this world, and he didn't deserve to die the way he did."

"He sounds like he was a great man," Hayden suggested.

"He was. One of the best I'd ever met." The only problem had been that he'd wanted me to move to London, and I hadn't wanted to give up everything I knew to go to a place I'd never experienced before. But he had a well-established life in London, and I had no one other than Morgan and a dead-end job I didn't even like very much. It only made sense that I'd be the one to move, but I'd been scared. It had been the one and only argument we'd ever gotten into.

"There are more men like him out there, I promise," Hayden said, taking my hand and holding it tightly.

"Men like you?"

He laughed dryly and shook his head. "No, I'm a bastard. I'm very envious of him for getting to you before I could. When it's all said and done, love, I don't deserve you a bit. I do stupid shit and get myself into even more stupid situations. I've done a lot of things I regret, and then some things I should regret but don't. If I wasn't so selfish, I'd tell you to run for your fucking life. But I *am* selfish, and I'm not ready to let you go."

I took his words in and turned them over in my head. He was warning me, but all I could think was how perfectly matched we were. Both screwed up in our own ways, but still holding on to whatever it was that was going on between us.

"I'm not scared of you, you know," I finally said.

"I know you aren't, and it attracts me to you even more."

Before I could change my mind, I climbed into his lap and straddled him.

He let out a deep sigh when I settled onto him. "What are you doing, love?"

"Working on that whole moving on with my life thing."

And then I pressed my lips to his, putting all my emotion and feeling behind it. When his hands rested on my hips, I deepened the kiss. We kissed for hours, holding each other close until it got too late for me to stay awake. The last thing I remembered was laying my head in his lap while he stroked my hair, and I was out.

Chapter Nine

I was tired the next morning from my late night, but it had been worth it. Hayden hadn't pushed for more than I'd been willing to give. After letting go of some of my pain, kissing him had come easier, and I didn't quite feel like I had a thousand-pound weight strapped to my heart anymore.

Though I knew I'd fallen asleep on the couch, I'd woken up in my bed. I figured either Hayden had moved me or I'd sleepwalked into bed at some point. I felt like I was riding high after the night I'd had. I'd taken one step closer to healing, and that was a big deal for me all things considered. Talking things out with Hayden had also done me a world of good.

I was just finishing folding some laundry when my phone beeped.

U and me, tonight, Club Rogue. Dancing, drinking, flirting. R U in?

I mulled it over some. It had been a while since I'd gone out with Morgan on a weekend. We had after-work drinks sometimes, but it wasn't the same as spending the night out on the town.

I'm in, I answered back.

I spent the rest of my day doing housework, hoping I'd hear from Hayden, but I hadn't exactly gone out of my way to message him either. By seven o'clock I was dressed and ready to go. I offered to drive tonight since my car had sputtered back to life, so I made the short drive to her place. She lived in a cute little bungalow in the artsy district of town, and I absolutely adored her house. It was painted a mint green with white trim and shutters, and the roof was pitched, giving the small house a bigger feel.

Beeping the horn to let her know I'd arrived, I checked my lip gloss in the visor mirror. Morgan came bounding down the porch steps in a slinky golden dress that barely covered her behind and climbed in.

"Ready for a night of dancing? I'm going to dance until I drop," she informed me. "I hope you've come prepared."

"I don't think I'll ever be able to keep up with you, but I'll certainly try." I laughed, and we pulled away. "Have you been to this place yet?"

She shook her head. "No, not yet, but I've heard good things. A couple of people I work with went last weekend and said it's definitely the place to be on a Saturday night."

If that was the case, I knew it was going to be packed. The thought of strangers' sweating bodies pressed up against me from every angle wasn't very appealing, but I was still going to go, if only for Morgan. I'd do nearly anything for her if it meant she'd be happy.

We had to circle the parking lot twice before we found a spot at the far end. When we got out of the car Morgan squealed, took my hand, and pulled me toward the doors. There was a line a mile long, and I suddenly wished I'd brought something to occupy me while we stood there. It was going to be a long wait if the impatient foot tapping of the people around us said anything about it.

"So, how are things going with Hayden?" she asked after we took our place at the back of the line.

My cheeks flushed as I remembered last night and how

he'd kissed me for hours. I could have spent many more hours kissing him, truth be told. He was by far the best kisser I'd experienced, and that led me to wonder what else he excelled in.

"You're totally blushing! Did you finally sleep with him?"

"No, we just kissed. A lot." I sighed with longing, wondering what he was up to on a Saturday night. Probably with his friends doing something sketchy, if I was being honest with myself. That made me think of Jade. Was she currently throwing herself at him, trying to seduce him into her bed? I immediately shook the thought from my head. Hayden had told me they were just friends, and I needed to believe him, otherwise I was going to go crazy.

"That's a step in the right direction, though, right?"

"Yeah, we talked about Drake a little, and, I don't know, it was like a part of me that was holding on so tightly to him let go some. Enough for me to feel comfortable with someone else. But I still couldn't bring myself to sleep with him yet. I don't know if I'll ever be ready for that." I couldn't very well expect him to hold out forever. Eventually he'd grow tired of the walls I'd put up and move on. Unless I found a way past them, and I didn't know what the likelihood of that was.

"Well, I think it's great that you're trying, Juliet." She squeezed my hand with a smile.

We continued to inch forward.

We finally made it inside the building, and my feet were already killing me from standing for so long. I convinced Morgan to sit at the bar with me for a moment to order drinks. I scanned the room, and a few lingering glances came in our direction, but I ignored them all.

After a drink, Morgan pulled me from the stool and dragged me to the dance floor. A thumping, monotonous beat pulsed from the speakers while a DJ stood inside a booth controlling the music. I quickly got into it, swaying my hips and raising my arms over my head. We danced for a long time to song after song, although they all sounded the same to me. Periodically, someone brushed my arm or back and I'd move into Morgan more.

"Let's go get another drink," Morgan yelled over the music. "I'm so thirsty."

I nodded and followed her off the dance floor.

We sat on stools once more in front of the bar and put in our drink orders. I let my gaze drift over the room, amazed at how full this place was. It was almost hard to believe they weren't violating some kind of fire marshal code. All I knew was that it felt good to sit down. Our drinks came, and we both took long gulps to quench our thirst.

"Look over there." Morgan pointed to a couple in leather in the corner of the room.

I found them very brave to wear something so form-fitting and revealing in such a crowded place. I'd never have the courage to do something like that. Morgan turned to pick her drink up again and threw it back, downing it all in one go, so I did the same.

"Let's just sit here a minute. It's hot as hell out there on the floor," she said.

I nodded my agreement as we sat back against the bar and took in the scene before us. There were couples dancing, making out, grinding into one another. It was like intimacy on display, but I found that it didn't bother me to see it. If anything, it filled me with a longing so strong that I thought about Hayden.

He was definitely being patient with me, only taking what I was able to give without asking for more. It seemed so at odds with his naturally abrasive personality. He was involved in some dark things that I'd never give a second thought to, but he was so gentle with me. More facets of his personality opening themselves to me. I wanted to think that maybe he trusted me with that side of him. I had this feeling he didn't show it to just anyone.

I was so lost in thought that when Morgan clutched my arm I jumped. "I don't feel so good."

"What's wrong" I asked, concern creasing my face.

"I-I don't know. I just feel really woozy and everything is blurry."

"Do you want to go home?" I hopped off the barstool and planted myself in front of her to help her up.

Her legs buckled beneath her, and I struggled to help her up.

"Do you need some help?" a guy asked, coming up to where I was huddled over Morgan.

"No, thanks, I've got it," I replied, not giving him any more thought.

"Seriously, let me help," he insisted.

"I said I've got it," I snapped and put my hand up to stop him.

I wrapped my arm around Morgan's waist and tried to lift her, but it was useless. I desperately searched around me to see if a bouncer was close by who could help me, but they were all too far away to hear me. There was no way I was leaving her here alone. She let out a small moan, and her eyes fluttered back before she went fully limp in my arms. Panicking, I pulled my cell from my purse and dialed the first number I could think of.

"Hello, gorgeous," Hayden answered.

"Hayden," I yelled over the music, my voice breaking in fear.

"What's wrong? Where are you?"

"I'm at Club Rogue with Morgan. I don't know what happened, but she just passed out, and I can't move her." I had no idea if he could even make out what I was saying over the loud music and my wavering voice, but I had to try.

"Hold on, I'll be there in ten."

The line went dead, and I moved closer to Morgan, trying to protect her from being trampled, keeping an eye on the door for Hayden.

Ten minutes later he was walking through the doors, casting his gaze around. When he spotted me sitting on the floor under the bar, he headed straight for us and crouched.

"You okay, love?"

I started to nod but then shook my head. "I want to leave," I wailed, wiping my nose with the back of my hand.

Hayden scooped Morgan up in his arms with ease, and we beelined toward the exit. Out in the fresh night air, I sucked in a breath and tried to calm myself down. Something had gone wrong, and I hoped Morgan was going to be okay. I didn't know what was going on, but I was scared.

"Where'd you park?" he asked.

I pointed to the end of the lot, and we made our way to the car. Hayden laid Morgan along the back seat and took my keys. He stopped me as I was about to climb into the car and pulled me into his chest, holding me tightly to him, pressing a kiss to the top of my head.

"Let's get you home, yeah?"

"Shouldn't we take her to a hospital or something?"

He glanced down before answering. "You do know she was drugged, right? There isn't much they'll be able to do. She just needs to sleep it off."

"Drugged?" I could hardly believe it, but nothing else made sense. She'd been perfectly fine while we were drinking at the bar, and then she suddenly wasn't. I swallowed hard as I looked at the passed-out form of my best friend lying in the backseat of my car.

Hayden opened the passenger door for me, and I slid in, still in shock.

The ride to my house was quiet, and I could do nothing but think of what could have happened tonight if I hadn't been with Morgan. She could have been hurt. Someone could have done something horrible to her.

When we got to my place, Hayden carried her up the two flights of stairs to my apartment. I told him to put Morgan in my bed as I paced the living room. Never in all the times we'd gone out to the bar had anything like this happened. I hadn't wanted to go to that stupid club in the first place and now I wished I'd convinced Morgan to go somewhere else.

"She should feel a little better by tomorrow."

I stopped pacing and looked across the room to where Hayden stood in the mouth of the short hallway. I rushed to him and threw my arms around him, burying my head in his chest.

"Thank you," I said, a muffled whisper against his shirt.

"No need to thank me, love. I'm glad you called me."

He put his arms around me, and we stood interlocked for a long moment. I breathed him in, instantly feeling safer.

His voice was gruff when he spoke again. "Could've been you."

"Hm?"

"It could've been you who got drugged."

He was right. It easily could have been me, but it wasn't. And I knew Morgan would have done everything in her power to get me to safety like I had for her.

"I'm fine, Hayden. I promise."

He wrapped his hand up in my curls and pulled gently, lifting my face to his. His mouth slanted over mine roughly, his tongue pressing between my lips to tangle with mine. When he broke away his breathing was ragged and harsh.

"Promise me you'll be careful if you go out again."

My knees felt weak from the unexpected kiss, my own breath coming sharply.

"I will."

He nodded once and stroked my cheek with the tips of his fingers. Almost as if involuntarily, I pressed my face into his hand and closed my eyes. It felt right being here with him in his arms. So right that I almost forgot why I'd felt any guilt at all for kissing him last night. It was a struggle, but I wanted this. I wanted to let go enough to enjoy whatever this thing was that was going on between Hayden and me. I just hoped that if I leaped off the cliff I was standing on, he'd be there at the bottom to catch me. And I hoped like hell everyone was right and Drake would want me to move on.

As if sensing my turmoil, he smiled a little and captured my chin between his fingers. "I'm not going to push you into anything you aren't ready for, love. I'm content to just kiss those sweet lips."

Desire swirled in me as his gaze locked on to my lips.

I wasn't sure how much longer I would be able to deny myself what I knew I really wanted. I barely knew anything at all about Hayden. He could be a player and would drop off the face of the earth after I slept with him for all I knew. But I didn't think I'd be content with just kissing him forever. I wanted more than that, even if the remorse for letting go of Drake for that moment would swallow me up afterward. I thought that I could deal with the fallout. I had to know what kind of lover Hayden was. Would he be sweet and sensual, or would he be rough and attentive? I was pretty certain I'd be fine with either of those options.

But Morgan was passed out in the next room, and this wasn't how I wanted it to happen. If I went through with it, if I slept with him, I wanted it to be in a better environment than this. It had been years since I'd last been with someone. I didn't want my first time in years to be against a wall or on my couch. Ideally, I wanted to be comfortable.

"Can you just hold me for a while?" I asked, hoping he

would oblige. I was still pretty shaken by Morgan blacking out at my feet and the realization that she'd been drugged, so being safe in his arms had its appeal.

"Absolutely," he answered without a second thought.

We moved to the couch, where he pulled me down into his lap and cradled me as if I were something precious. It felt better than it probably should have.

"Will Morgan really be okay?" She was dead to the world right now, sleeping soundly not even fifteen feet away.

"She'll be really groggy when she wakes, but I promise you she's going to be fine. Are you going to be okay, though?"

I thought it through before I answered. I was rattled by the events of the night, and probably scarred for life as far as nightclubs went. I wouldn't be going there again anytime soon, or ever for that matter. But Morgan was somewhere safe where no one could hurt her, I was home, and I was in Hayden's arms.

"I think so, yes. I just don't know how I'm going to break the news to Morgan tomorrow about what happened to her. I think if someone told me I was drugged at a club I'd probably lose my mind." Morgan was the strongest person I knew, but that didn't mean it wouldn't be crushing to know someone tried taking advantage of her. "Can I ask you something?"

"What is it?"

Before I could change my mind, I asked, "Why are you so nice to me? You could have anyone you wanted, and I know I'm not really your type. Our worlds don't collide in any way, and I want to make sure that I'm not just some game to you."

"I don't think you're a game at all, love. I'm nice to you because I like you and I want to know you better. I'm not fucking around with you." He brought his mouth to my ear.

"And while I know I could go find someone else's knickers to get into, I'd much rather find myself in yours."

My heart skipped a beat. It was hard to resist him when he talked to me like that. His voice, thickly accented and heated, proved his desire for me was real. That along with the hard length beneath me that only continued to grow.

"So, you really do want me then?" It was a redundant question. I could *feel* how much he wanted me. Words could mean very little sometimes, but the proof was pressing right against my backside.

"Very much so." His fingers lazily traced circles over my collarbone, and he continued speaking. "While I'm willing to wait until you're ready for more, I can't deny that I haven't thought about dragging you off to your bedroom and having my way with you every time I've come to your door. I wonder what sounds you'd make when I have my mouth on you or when I'm buried inside you, and I wonder what face you'll make right when you're on the brink of coming. Do you want to know how many times I've had to get myself off thinking about you this week alone?"

I pulled back and looked him in the eye. A spark ignited in his pitch-black irises, and I knew that before this was all said and done, I'd be in bed with him. I couldn't keep stalling while maintaining my sanity.

"I've thought of you, too," I admitted, my face warming with a deep blush.

"Judging by that adorable heat to your cheeks, I'd say they weren't innocent thoughts."

"Not entirely pure," I agreed, drawing my finger over the lines of his shirt.

"Tell me your greatest fantasy."

I couldn't believe I was about to say it out loud. I'd never been one to openly talk about fantasies and sex, but I wanted to tell him. This verbal foreplay would make the real thing even better when the time finally came.

"My greatest fantasy," I repeated. "I think that would have to be being restrained in some way. I always have so much control over myself and the situations I'm in that the idea of trusting someone enough to give up that control feels . . . exciting."

His eyes darkened, and I knew he was imagining me tied up in bed, his to do with as he pleased. Just the thought alone sent a wet rush through me, and my panties dampened. His eyes closed briefly, and when they opened, there was a carnal hardness to them that nearly took my breath away.

"If I had my way . . ." He trailed off.

I waited for him to finish his sentence, but he never did. "What about you? What's your greatest fantasy?"

He didn't even think about it before opening his mouth and letting the words tumble out. "Right now, my greatest fantasy would be knowing what you taste like."

My mouth dropped open as I fought the urge to throw caution to the wind and shred his clothes from his body. I squirmed around in his lap, and he grunted.

"You're killing me, love."

It dawned on me that I'd been rubbing myself against his hard-on, and I stuttered an apology. "S-sorry. I wasn't thinking."

"No, your problem is that you think *too* much. It's okay to let yourself go every now and then, let yourself just feel." He brushed my hair back and kissed my cheek so tenderly.

"I'm trying to. I-I think I'm ready."

He ceased to move, taking in what I was saying. "What are you ready for?"

"For, well, you know," I said, dancing around the answer.

"I want to hear you say it," he replied, that same gruff growl breaking free from his chest.

I gathered up all the courage I had and didn't look away when I said, "I'm ready to sleep with you."

"No, there will be no sleeping involved. You're ready to fuck me, yeah?"

I nodded slowly. My body was humming, begging me to get on with it. It had been waiting so long for me to admit out loud that I wanted him as much as he'd said he wanted me.

Hayden slid me off his lap and stood. I drew my brows in, watching him rub his hand across his face. Had I said something wrong?

"If Morgan wasn't here, I'd take your sweet ass to bed right now, but I'm afraid we're going to have to wait just a little longer. Tomorrow afternoon, I'll come pick you up. I want to take you somewhere, and then I'm bringing you back here." He crouched so he was at eye level with me. "And when I do, I'm going to make damn sure you don't regret letting me into your bed."

"Hayden," I whispered, reaching out and pressing my palm to his cheek.

He turned his face to press a kiss into my hand before leaning forward and planting a searing kiss on my lips.

Standing upright once more, he looked down at me. "I need to plan for tomorrow, but if you need me, just call. I'll be here."

I stood on shaking legs and followed him to the door to lock it behind him. Once he stepped through, he turned to me and wrapped his hand around the back of my neck. Pulling me into the wettest, most explosive kiss yet, he then said against my lips, "Tomorrow."

"Tomorrow," I confirmed.

He was smiling as he turned and jogged down the stairs.

I locked the door and leaned into it. I had just signed my fate, decided to place my trust in him for at least one night.

My heart raced uncontrollably when I slipped into my room to change for bed as quietly as I could manage so I wouldn't wake Morgan. I was really going to go through with this. I was going to give myself to someone for the first time in years.

It went without saying that I was beyond anxious, my stomach rolling with nervous energy. There was a moment of panic when I nearly called him to cancel, but I quickly decided against it. I was scared to death, but I wanted it. Calling him to cancel would just make everyone right. I didn't take risks, ever. And Hayden would be one of the biggest risks I could take. Because of that, I knew I had to do this for myself.

I unlocked my phone and pulled up my photos. There saved in my photos was a picture of Drake he'd sent me two days before he'd died. His blond hair glowed in the sun like a halo, and his emerald eyes sparkled as he looked right into the camera. He was smiling, showing off his perfect teeth, and I found myself smiling back before my smile died altogether. If I slept with Hayden like I knew I was going to, I'd be letting go of Drake even more than I already had. Miss Caroline was right, I'd never forget him, everything led back to thoughts of him, but I was starting to think that maybe moving on wasn't as bad as I'd thought it would be. I was still carrying the pain of letting go, though, and I wasn't sure that would go away.

I kissed the picture and held my phone to my chest while tears slipped from my eyes.

"I'm sorry, Drake," I whispered into the air, not for the first time since meeting Hayden. "Please forgive me."

Chapter Ten

I was sitting on a chair by the window with a cup of coffee when Morgan came padding into the living room.

"Oh God. I feel like I've been run over by the entire Macy's Day Parade," she complained, throwing herself onto the couch.

I stared at her uneasily. I had to tell her what happened, even if it meant she would probably freak out. She deserved to know.

"There's something I need to tell you," I said and sat straighter in my chair.

"What?" She was using a makeup remover wipe to wash her face. "Why did you let me go to sleep wearing my makeup? You know I hate that shit."

I chewed on the inside of my cheek. "You were passed out before we made it back."

"How did you manage to get me up here? No offense, but I have at least four inches on you and I know there's no way you managed to carry me with those toothpick arms."

I needed to just spit it out. The longer I drew this out, the worse it was going to be.

"Hayden carried you for me."

She shot me a confused look, so I pressed on.

"We were having a drink by the bar and, well, you said you didn't feel well and passed out. I called Hayden to help me get you to the car, and he brought you up to my room. We think someone might have drugged you."

A thick silence fell over us as Morgan registered what I'd

said. Shock won out, and her eyes rounded. "I guess that explains why I don't remember anything."

"I'm so sorry, Morgan. I should have been paying better attention to our drinks. Maybe then that wouldn't have happened."

She shook her head adamantly. "Don't you dare put this on yourself. It was a shitty thing for someone to do to me, but you kept me safe." Her voice broke, tears pushing through. "I could have . . . someone could have . . ."

She let the rest of her sentence hang in the air, and we both envisioned the worst. Someone could have hurt her unimaginably. I moved to the couch and pulled her into my arms. As soon as her head fell onto my shoulder, sobs rocked her body, and I held her until she was done crying.

"Thank you for making sure nothing happened to me," she sniffled, pulling back and rubbing at her eyes.

Morgan didn't show her emotions freely with everyone. Only a select few in her life got that softer side of her, and I was one of those lucky few.

"I love you, Morgan. I'd never let anything happen to you."

"I love you, too, Juliet."

We sat together for a while talking about how we were never going to Club Rogue again when my phone beeped. I stared at the message.

Be ready by noon.

My stomach lurched with anticipation. I had an hour before he was here. Jumping to my feet, I glanced at Morgan and knew the panic had to be clear on my face when she said, "Where's the fire?"

"Hayden is going to be here in an hour, and I haven't even showered!"

"Have plans?" She smiled mischievously.

"Big plans," I said, trying to emphasize just how big those plans were.

"You're going to finally sleep with him, aren't you? About damn time." She stood and went to the door, slipping her heels back on. "I'm out of here. Go get ready and tell me all about it when you come out of the sex cave." Then her face fell. "I don't have my car."

"Take mine, and I'll come by to get it later."

She grabbed up my keys off the kitchen counter and pecked me on the cheek.

"Have fun, and don't do anything I wouldn't do."

Her singsong voice echoed in my head long after she shut the door behind her. I rushed to the bathroom to take a quick shower, running a razor over my legs, and then I stood naked in front of my closet with a towel on my head.

I sifted through my clothes, finally deciding on a black long-sleeved sweater dress with leggings under it. I was just pulling my ankle boots on when there was a knock. I quickly made my way to the door, taking a deep breath for courage. I unlocked and opened it. When I appeared in the doorway, he appraised me slowly as if trying to remember every curve of my body. It had the incredible effect of making me feel stripped naked, though that wouldn't come until later.

"Hello, beautiful." He stepped closer to me and pulled me in against his chest. "You smell good."

"That's what happens when you take a shower," I said facetiously.

He snorted. "Smartass."

I couldn't help but laugh when he kissed the top of my head and let me go.

"Come on, let's go," he said.

He held my hand, dragging me along until we stood in front of a sleek black SUV. I came up short, my gaze darting between Hayden and the massive vehicle.

"Whose is this?"

"It's mine," he said as if it should have been obvious.

"Where's the bike?"

He pulled the passenger door open for me, and I climbed in.

"Miss it, do you?"

I might have. Just a little.

"No, just curious," I half lied. "Where did you get this anyway?"

He waited until he came around to the driver's seat and got in behind the wheel to answer. "Don't ask and I won't have to tell you."

Alarmed, I shrieked, "Did you steal it?"

He barked out a laugh and gave me a pointed stare. "It depends on your definition of stealing."

I jerked on the handle, but the door was locked. "Let me out of this car right now, or I swear to God, Hayden . . ."

"Relax, love, I didn't steal it." He snickered, trying to hide his smile and failing miserably.

"If we get stopped by the cops for grand theft auto, I'm telling them you kidnapped me," I warned, only making him laugh harder.

"They have to find us first."

His eyes flashed with excitement, and I shook my head in disbelief. He was insane. I crossed my arms over my chest and grumbled while he backed the car out of the spot and drove away.

Five minutes later we stopped at a light, and he glanced over at me. "Are you still mad at me?"

"I'm not mad, I'm irritated. Big difference." I wasn't even irritated anymore. Instead I was dangling right over a pit of anticipation for what the rest of my day held. I knew how this was going to end, and I was mentally trying to prepare myself for it.

"Ah, don't be irritated. I was only joking."

"Then tell me where you got it from," I asked, making a point to look him right in the eye.

"I won it," he simply said.

"You won it?"

"Yes, and that's all you need to know."

End of discussion. Maybe he hadn't stolen it per se, but he hadn't come across it by innocent means either—his tone implied as much. So I dropped it. I didn't really want to know the details.

When we stopped in a spot across from the park, I raised a brow.

"Just trust me," he said with a sly smile.

I hopped out, and he grabbed a bag from the backseat. Taking my hand, he led me across the road into the park. We walked along the pathway for a bit before we stopped at a secluded area surrounded by a thicket of trees and bushes that once held leaves and flowers. It seemed a little cold for a day at the park, but at least the wind wasn't blowing.

He laid a blanket out and gestured for me to sit, then threw himself down next to me. He stretched out, propping his head up in his hand, appraising me again, biting down on his lip. The intensity of his stare made me shift around, but I couldn't get comfortable with him watching me like that. My skin tingled, and a deep pull began in my belly, ending right between my legs.

"Come here." He beckoned with a crook of his finger.

I slid over to him, and he dragged me the rest of the way into him. He nuzzled my neck, his hand wandering over my shoulder, down my side, and he brushed over my breast, down to my hip. I shivered against his touch, and a soft moan bubbled up from within my throat.

"Hayden," I whispered, "what if someone sees us?"

"Makes it exciting, doesn't it?"

I must have made a horrified face because he smiled and said, "No one else is here. It's just us."

I relaxed a degree but couldn't let go completely. His hand was burning into my hip where it rested searing his fingertips into me.

Then his hand went lower. His fingers danced along my thigh, stroking the skin through my leggings. When they trailed to the inside of my thigh, leaving the softest touch, my legs shook. Hayden's tongue darted out along my neck, just below my ear in that sensitive spot that melted my insides completely.

"I want to touch you, love," he rasped over my skin.

Without a word, I spread my legs farther apart, hardly believing I was about to do this in a public park. His fingers continued moving slowly toward my center, leaving a trail of scorched flesh in their wake. I was sure I'd stopped breathing.

When he palmed me between my legs, a strangled cry left me. It had been so long since someone had touched me there, and I suddenly wondered why I'd waited years to feel this again. He rubbed gently at first, teasing me with his fingers, so I ground myself into his hand.

"Greedy girl," he murmured, continuing to suck on my neck.

His mouth came to mine, capturing my lips in a warm kiss that only aided in frustrating me further.

"Shut up," I said against his lips and I could feel him smile.

His hand left my center and traveled up my sweater dress, where he dragged his fingers along the waistband of my leggings. The skin-to-skin contact was almost more than I could handle, and I wriggled around beneath him.

His hand slipped under the waistband, and he toyed with the elastic of my panties before continuing to explore. When his fingers brushed my swollen clit through my panties, I yelped and jerked my hips. He didn't cease his exploration, moving farther down, and he groaned.

"You're soaked, babe."

I could feel how wet I was, drenched from his unrelenting teasing. If it weren't for being in a public area, I'd have already begged him to take me right here. Screw his plans for the day when I needed to come, needed to know what he felt like inside me.

But all too soon he pulled his hand away, out of my leggings, and left a light kiss on my lips. "Hungry?"

"Not for food," I griped.

He chuckled before sitting up. He jerked the bag closer and got out some sandwiches, fruits, nuts, and drinks. "I guess you'll just have to wait. Pity."

I shot him a dirty look and I sat up, folding my legs beneath me. My legs were still shaking, almost feeling his fingers on me even now.

"You're cute when you're sexually frustrated."

"And you're the Devil," I answered, taking a sandwich from his outstretched hand.

"I've been called worse," he said with a smirk.

I rolled my eyes, biting into the sandwich.

"How was Morgan this morning?" he asked.

I sobered up immediately. "She was really upset when I told her what happened. She seemed okay when she left, but I need to check on her soon to make sure. I don't want her to deal with it on her own. She's been seeing this guy at work, but honestly, he doesn't really seem like the reliable type when it comes to listening and offering comfort during a hard time." Mark wasn't a horrible guy from what I knew of him, but he also wasn't the best. He was in it all for the fun, and Morgan knew as well as I did that the first time someone else caught his attention, he'd cast her off in a heartbeat.

I didn't know how she dealt with knowing that, but then I realized I couldn't say much. Hayden could do the same to me, for all I knew. The fun was in the anticipation. How would he treat me once he'd finally had me?

"Call her when we're done with lunch, check in."

I nodded, my mood quickly going sour as those creeping doubts settled in. I had to admit I was worried that if I slept with him then I wouldn't hear from him again, and try as I might to deny it, he was growing on me. Sure, he had his issues and was into some shady dealings, but he was kind to me, showered me with affection.

"Something on your mind?"

I looked up from my plate of strawberries. "Nope." I should have been honest. I should have told him my worries so I at least knew what this was. But I couldn't bring myself to do it.

"Liar," he accused.

I sighed and avoided his probing stare. "It's nothing. It's just my own crap that I need to deal with."

"Drake?" he asked, and I flinched at the reminder.

"That's part of it, I suppose. But I'm finding it a little easier."

"And the other part?"

It was now or never, I told myself. If I got this awkward what-am-I-to-you conversation out of the way now, it would be much better in the long run. Then I could walk away from this if I was nothing more than a one-night stand. I wasn't ready to do something like that, even for Hayden.

"What . . . I guess I just want to know if I'm going to hear from you again after tonight. You aren't obligated to stick around, you don't owe me anything, but I'm not ready for some brief one-time thing. If that's what you want, then I think we need to go ahead and end this before anything more happens. Even if I want it, I can't do that to myself.

And—"

He put a finger to my lips to cease my rambling. "You think I'm just going to fuck you and disappear?"

Slowly I shrugged and looked down at my hands.

"I've done questionable things, but I'm not an asshole. I know the type who wants only that, and I know you aren't it. I've told you before, if all I wanted was a one-time thing, I would have left you alone and gone searching for that instead. Have little faith, love."

A surge of relief came over me, and I was glad then that I'd mustered up the courage to say something. I was almost embarrassed, though, for nearly accusing him of only playing with my feelings. I didn't love him, but I did like him, and after months of loneliness, I really needed something good in my life. I didn't know how things would play out, but I wanted to see where it went. If he'd been here a month already, he only had about two months left until he'd be forced to leave. My options were to either end things before they'd ever truly begun or accept a couple of months and learn to let go when the time came, and I wasn't ready to end things just yet.

After lunch I stepped away to call Morgan while Hayden cleaned up from our picnic. I smiled thinking only he would be crazy to have a picnic in winter, but I had enjoyed it, even in the cold. Though now my nose was probably red and frozen, and my fingers felt like ice cubes. I'd stupidly left my gloves at home, but I hadn't realized I'd need them.

Once I'd talked to Morgan and made sure she was doing all right, or as okay as she could be considering, I made my way back over to Hayden who was waiting on me.

"Everything fine?"

"She'll survive, I think," I answered.

He leaned down to slide his lips along mine. "Ready to go to your place?"

Flutters of desire swept through me again while my stomach turned somersaults. Without saying a word, I took his hand and pulled him to the jeep.

The ride to my apartment was filled with unbridled tension. Hayden held my hand, rubbing his thumb in circles that only aided in making me more nervous. When he touched me, I felt it in my whole body — even something as simple as his thumb tracing lines across my hand.

I was really going to do this, and I was putting Drake in the back of my mind for the time being. He would come back to haunt me at some point, and I hoped that I was ready for when he did. For now, I was going to take a risk and I was going to go after what I wanted.

CHAPTER ELEVEN

I stuck my key in the lock and twisted, and my insides twisted along with it. I let us into the apartment and locked the door behind us, buying time before I had to face him. When I turned around, he was staring at me with an intensity I wasn't sure I could match.

Prowling over to me like I was his prey, Hayden captured my wrist in his hand and led me toward the bedroom. I looked at my bed, still turned down from where Morgan and I had slept last night. I hadn't had time to make it up before he'd arrived today.

He pulled me against him, his hardness pressing into my belly while his mouth slanted over mine, his hands resting right at my lower back, holding me to him. I put my palms on his chest and gripped his shirt between my fingers as his trailed lower to the hem of my sweater dress. He broke the kiss long enough to lift it up over my head and cast it to the floor. Hayden backed me up until I tumbled onto the bed. His gaze never left mine as he removed my boots.

Grasping my leggings around the waistband, he tugged them off slowly, bending at the waist to plant kisses on the tops of my thighs, so close to where I really wanted his mouth. I lay there before him in nothing but my underclothes, and I'd never felt so exposed in my life.

"You're shaking, love. Are you scared?"

Yes, terrified.

"No, not at all." The tremor in my voice betrayed me.

He climbed over me and put his forehead to mine.

"I'll take care of you, Juliet," he promised, briefly kissing my lips, following a path down to my chest. He kissed the swells of my breasts and reached behind me to undo the clasp on my bra. As it fell away, he leaned back to look down at me. "Perfect," he rasped.

When his mouth closed over my nipple, I cried out, and my hips undulated on their own. He bit down on it gently then sucked it back into his mouth while I writhed under him. He showed the same attention to my other nipple, and his mouth roamed lower to cascade kisses along my abdomen. His tongue dipped into my belly button, then teased the line just above the top of my panties. I was gasping for breath, my lungs constricted.

His fingers hooked into my panties, and he drew them down my legs until he was tossing them across the room. Returning his attention to my body, he spread my legs with his hands and ran his rough fingers down the insides of my thighs, stopping right before reaching the one spot I needed him to touch.

"God, you're beautiful, Juliet. Every fucking inch of you."

He looked lost, his eyes glazed over with want and need. He glanced up at me through his dark lashes, lowering his head to my body once more. He kissed the top of my mound and continued lower. At the first touch of his tongue on my clit, I moaned loudly and dug my hands into his hair.

He groaned, sending vibrations through me as he laved me over and over again. I already felt close to falling apart under his tongue, but then his hand snaked up between us, and his fingers teased my entrance. At a maddening pace he pushed one finger inside me, then two. Curling his fingers up to that sensitive spot, he continued to lick me into a frenzied puddle of unintelligible cries.

"Hayden, I-I'm . . ."

He jerked away suddenly, taking his tongue and fingers

with him. I whimpered for more.

"Not yet, love. You come with me." He stood, removing his clothes from his body.

I watched through hooded eyes as he revealed his taut body to me. His strong arms came into focus, followed by his chiseled abdomen. Then he cast off his pants and boxers, his erection springing forward. It was long, hard, and red in its anticipation for what was about to happen.

Hayden dug around for something in the pocket of his jeans, a condom, and ripped it open with his teeth. He stared down at me, rolling it on and pitching forward onto the bed again, positioning himself over me.

"Ready?" he asked.

I nodded furiously. "Please, Hayd—" But my begging was cut off abruptly by the head of his cock pressing into me. "Oh my God," I whispered in a strangled voice when he pushed farther in.

His breathing was heavy, the corded muscles of his arms straining. When he was fully seated inside me, he stopped moving and closed his eyes. "Heaven," he rumbled.

"More," I begged him.

His lips tilted up on one side. "Tell me what you want, love." He rocked his hips lazily, teasing me with what he knew I needed.

"Anything," I pleaded. Still, he kept going at his unhurried pace. "Please, Hayden. Please just fuck me."

That seemed to be the answer he was waiting for. He drew back and thrust gently. He rested his elbows on either side of my head, his body flush with mine, kissing me deeply. He was awakening in me things I hadn't even been aware I'd been missing until this moment. It was drawing out something primitive from deep within. Still, his gentle rhythm wasn't enough for me. I could take whatever he had to give.

"Harder," I pleaded.

Something flashed quickly in his eyes before a dark gleam took over. "Are you sure?"

To answer him I lifted myself to my elbows and kissed him roughly, biting at his bottom lip. He grunted and shoved me back down, then slammed his hips into me with more force than before. I clutched at his biceps as he met me halfway, lifting my hips to reach him, with thrusts so deep I could feel it in my whole body.

I babbled his name over and over again, my eyes rolling back while I edged closer to the precipice of total bliss. His mouth found mine, and he delved his tongue inside, continuing to thrust. The sounds of our harsh breathing and our skin meeting filled the room. I was flying high, ready for the crash.

"Hayden, I'm close," I murmured when his lips found mine.

"Come, love," he commanded.

He leaned back, my legs suspended in the air between us, and stuck his fingers to my clit. He rubbed it quickly, driving his hips into mine. I clutched the sheets on either side of me, thrashing my head back and forth.

Moments later my body exploded into a million little pieces, and I leaped from that ledge, plummeting into ecstasy. I came around him on a loud, drawn-out moan, his name immediately following. My voice was hoarse and broken from the sheer power of my orgasm.

I held on just long enough for Hayden to follow me over. He closed his eyes and tumbled into his own orgasm, whispering my name gutturally. I'd never in my life seen anything sexier than the look on his face as he shook. When he stilled inside me, my body went limp, and he rested his head on my chest. I brought up an exhausted arm and ran my fingers through his thick dark hair. He sprinkled kisses on my chest and raised his head, our eyes locking.

"Goddamn, woman," he rasped.

"What?"

"If only I'd have met you when I first got here. I could have had this sweet pussy all to myself a long time ago."

His cock jerked inside me, and I quivered under him, my legs still shaking from coming so powerfully.

I smiled and kissed his forehead tenderly. Reluctantly he pulled out and left me lying there while he went to dispose of the condom. I sighed and stared at the ceiling, sated for the first time in years. All this time I'd been pleasuring myself when someone like Hayden was walking around in the world. It seemed like such a shame.

The bed dipped inward when he came back and settled in next to me. He wasted no time pulling me into his side. We lay like that for a while, basking in the afterglow. My eyes fluttered, and I struggled to stay awake, but eventually I lost the battle and slipped into unconsciousness.

I woke to an empty bed and momentary panic that Hayden had upped and left, but then I spotted him by the window. I was tucked into the comforter, still naked. He'd put his boxers on, but the rest of his glorious body was on display. I watched him for a long while as he stared out the window.

Finally I said, "What are you looking at?"

He turned to me with a dimpled smile. "It's snowing." He came over to sit on the edge of the bed and brushed my hair back off my face.

I squinted through the open blinds, and sure enough, flakes of white were falling. The blanket slipped, so I jerked it back up, suddenly embarrassed about my nudity.

Hayden took the blanket from my hands and let it fall to expose my breasts. He thumbed one of my nipples, my body awakening to his touch.

"Don't hide from me, love. I want to see your body always."

His voice was so soft and packed with feeling that my heart ached.

I was just about to tell him that I wanted to share my body with him for as long as he'd have me, but there was a pounding on my front door. My brows drew together. I hadn't been expecting anyone. I scrambled from the bed, throwing on my pink satin robe. I was tying it off when I opened my door and Morgan stomped in.

"I'm going to kill him," she shrieked.

"Who?"

"Mark, who else? That bastard took me out to dinner just to break things off with me. A simple *hey, this isn't working* would have sufficed, but no, no he had to take me out to dinner and embarrass me in front of an entire restaurant."

Hayden came out of my bedroom, and Morgan's eyes rounded.

"Oh, sorry, I didn't realize you'd still be here."

He'd put on his pants but still stood there shirtless. Morgan looked between the two of us with a smirk. I silently begged her not to make a big deal of it.

"I'm not being irrational, am I?" she asked me. "I mean, I knew that things wouldn't last between us, but I think I deserved a little better than being made a fool of in front of a waiter."

"I'm sorry he did that. That wasn't the best way to handle things," I added supportively.

"You know why he left me? Shannon in sales shook her oversized ass at him one day. He even said as much. That he'd found someone else and he wasn't interested anymore. He's such a fucking cocksucker," she wailed.

I knew the tears were about to come, Hayden being present or not.

"You're better off," I stated. "Mark was an asshole, even on his best days."

Morgan put her head in her hands and sniffled. It didn't matter how many guys did this to her, she was always left angry over it. Morgan had had nothing but meaningless flings, but even I could tell she wasn't cut out for it. She needed something more stable, someone who wouldn't break her heart. And she deserved that much as well, even if she didn't believe in it.

I glanced at Hayden who was busy watching me. I wondered then if he was going to end up breaking my heart one of these days. We barely knew each other and had just slept together for the first time, but I knew the thoughts swirling in my head were dangerous. I could easily get attached to him if I wasn't careful.

"You want me to make you some tea and sit with you? We'll call Mark every name in the book and even do a spell to make his dick fall off," I suggested, trying to make her laugh.

"Remind me to never piss you off." Hayden laughed, which in turn had Morgan laughing.

"She seems all sweet and innocent, sure, but when she's mad, she's a force to reckon with. In the five years I've known her, I've seen her pissed off twice, and even I was scared of her."

Morgan was exaggerating as usual, but I let it slide because of her current woes.

"Duly noted," Hayden answered.

Morgan sighed and dropped her head. "I'm just going to go back home and eat an entire tub of ice cream in front of the TV. I should have called before I came over anyway." Morgan knew she never had to call before showing up at my place. There was an unspoken rule that we were always welcome in each other's homes. Hayden's being here didn't change that.

"You don't have to go, you know," I informed her. "If you need me, I'm here."

Morgan spared a glance in Hayden's direction. "No, no, I'm definitely leaving. You're . . . busy." She smiled and muttered under her breath, "Finally."

Hayden choked back a laugh, masking it as a cough.

I gave them both a glare and snapped, "Okay, that's enough about me."

"I'm just saying," Morgan began. "Call me later. We have a lot to talk about." She gave Hayden a two-finger salute, kissed me on the cheek, and left through the front door.

The snow was coming down harder, and I hoped she would be okay. I stuck my head out the door and called after her. "Let me know when you get home." I'd worry about her until I heard from her. After losing both my parents and Drake to car accidents, I was prone to worry. I sighed and pinched the bridge of my nose as I locked the door again.

"Poor girl can't catch a break, eh?"

Hayden pulled me into his arms, and I rested my head against his chest, listening to the steady thump of his heart.

"Not lately, it seems," I answered, truly feeling sorry for my best friend. Morgan was strong, and I knew she'd get past this like she had every time in the past, but it didn't mean I was any less concerned. Normally we would have crashed on my couch with a bottle of vodka and complained about men all night until she passed out. She didn't think she was welcome while Hayden was here, and that bothered me. Morgan came first before any guy, always. I'd remind her of that later when we talked again.

"You know what I'm thinking right now," Hayden asked, his voice rumbling low in his chest as he talked, seduction dripping from his lips.

"What?"

"I'm thinking about how very naked you are under that robe and I think we should take advantage of it."

Before I could speak my agreement, he lifted me off my feet into his arms and carried me to bed.

CHAPTER TWELVE

It was midday on Monday, and I was waiting in the lobby for Morgan so we could go to lunch. Proving his words to be the absolute truth, Hayden hadn't dropped off the face of the earth after we'd slept together. He'd been messaging me all morning, little teasing comments that made me wet while I sat at my desk, everyone around me none the wiser.

"I am *starving*," Morgan complained when she finally found me. "Let's go to the food truck. It's faster." In reality it really wasn't. We'd still have to wait in line regardless, but I knew Morgan could be unreasonable when she was hungry, so I agreed and followed her across the street.

We were standing in line when Morgan elbowed me in the side.

"Tell me how yesterday went, skank. Was he into any freaky shit?"

My face burned. "God, no, Morgan," I coughed out as I looked around to make sure no one was listening.

"Then give me *something*. My well has run dry as of yesterday, and I need to live vicariously through you now. I've decided I'm swearing off guys for a while."

I'd heard that one before but didn't remind her that she'd basically said it after every guy she'd ended things with.

"He was really nice. And attentive. It was by far the best I've ever had, hands down." I kept playing the day over in my head again and again. After that first time we'd hit the sheets twice more, the wall once, my dresser, and eventually my couch. I had to give him props for his stamina, give credit where credit was due. He'd done things to my body I'd only ever dreamed of.

"I'm so jealous. I know I'm better off in the long run. Mark was never very good in bed. Does Hayden have any friends?"

I rolled my eyes. "What happened to you swearing off men?" I raised an eyebrow in question.

"Just for future reference," she said with a shrug.

"Uh huh," I replied.

"Are you planning on still seeing him?"

"Yeah I think so. I mean, he's still talking to me, so I assume so. He said it wasn't a one-time thing for him, so I think that means he wants to see me again." I chewed my lip nervously. He'd assured me he wasn't into the one-night stand thing with me, but I still had that cloud of apprehension dangling over me. Something just didn't feel right, but I figured it was because he was mixed up in some bad stuff. It worried me a lot more than I let on. But I was a known worrier, so maybe I was overreacting.

"If he's still hitting you up after sleeping with you, he's still interested. Trust me."

And I did trust her wholly. If anyone knew anything about sex and men, it was Morgan.

We reached the window of the truck and ordered our sandwiches. While we waited, I checked my phone to see a message from Hayden.

Thinking about you wrapping your legs around me again. Debating on stealing you from work to take you to bed.

You're bad, Hayden. I can't leave work.

A man can dream.

I smiled down at my phone, and Morgan made a sound of

approval. "You're happy, aren't you?"

The question took me by surprise. I hadn't really considered it. I'd felt my guilt over Drake hovering right above me since this morning, but I tried shoving it down until later when I could be alone. Crying at work wasn't exactly something I wanted to be known for. "I think so," I said lamely.

"You don't smile like that ever anymore. It's nice seeing you smile again." Her voice had gone soft with emotion.

"Then I guess I am," I responded with a lift of my lips.

We grabbed our sandwiches from the window and took them back to the cafeteria in our work building. Snow had dusted over everything, making it impossible to sit outside.

Since Morgan had had my car, she'd picked me up for this morning, and I was planning on dropping her by her house after the day was over. I was a little nervous about driving in the snow, although I'd lived here for my whole life except for when I'd gone off to college and moved one town over. I should be used to the snow, but driving made me nervous even on a clear, sunny day.

We settled in at an empty table, and I had just taken a bite of my sandwich when someone sat next to me. I turned my head to come face to face with Carter.

"Tonight, can you work late? I have some extra files that I'd rather trust to you than someone else."

I gave him an apologetic look. "I'm Morgan's ride home tonight or I would. Can it wait until tomorrow night?"

"Sure. I'll put you down for tomorrow." He winked — my skin crawled — and left us alone once more.

"God, he creeps me out." Morgan made a face of disgust and took a bite.

"You and me both," I agreed. But I'd put off staying later to help out for a while, and if I wanted that upcoming raise, I needed to prove that I was reliable and flexible. So I'd stay tomorrow and power through having to work alongside

Carter.

After lunch, I sat at my desk fielding more texts from Hayden.

Can't wait to taste you again.

And why is that?

Because you taste like fucking Heaven.

I sighed with longing, wishing I could be with him instead of stuck at work. There was so much more I wanted to do with him. My phone vibrated with another message.

I'm busy tonight, but maybe tomorrow?

I have to work late tomorrow. Probably until about eight.

I'm not ninety years old, babe. I can stay up past eight.

Then tomorrow it is. Pick me up?

Sure thing. What floor?

12th. There's a lobby as soon as you walk in. Just wait there.

See you tomorrow, love.

He wanted to see me again. I couldn't stop the massive smile that overtook my face as I read his messages over again. Putting my phone away before I got caught, I tried focusing on my work.

When the end of the day finally came, I headed down to the garage and found my car. Morgan showed up minutes later and tossed the keys to me. We drove along, Morgan chattering away about her day, how excruciating it was working for her boss and how obnoxious Shelley's, the receptionist's, perfume was.

"So, when are you seeing Hottie with a Body again?" she asked, changing the subject.

"What did you just call him?"

"Oh, come on, I know he's off limits but I still have eyes, for fuck's sake."

I snorted in amusement and let her stew for a moment before answering. "Tomorrow night after I'm done helping Carter." I made a face as I said his name, showing my obvious distaste for having to stay late.

"Think of it as your reward for having to put up with that sleazeball. I'm so excited for you that you've finally broken your three-year dry spell. I feel like we should celebrate. We can go out to the Harbinger after work sometime this week."

I peeked at her from the corner of my eye, worried about going out again after what had happened last time, worried about her, but she showed no signs of anxiety over going out. Like I said, she was the strongest person I knew. I hoped that what happened at Club Rogue didn't haunt her like it did me. It wasn't even me it had happened to, but I still remembered the panic and fear I'd felt and I didn't think I'd forget it for a long time. I knew I'd be keeping an extra eye on my drinks from now on.

"Sure, we can go to the Harbinger later this week. Maybe Wednesday?"

"Yeah, if Hayden doesn't snatch you up first. I wouldn't even be mad. You have a lot of lost time to make up for."

I grumbled to myself as she beamed in her seat, clearly happy she could finally tease me about my sex life.

I dropped her off, flashing my lights as a goodbye, and drove home. Letting myself into my apartment, I slipped my shoes off and dropped my bag on the counter, poured myself a glass of wine and sat on the couch. Flipping through channels on the TV, I set my glass on the side table, and my picture of Drake caught my eye.

Instantly that guilt that had been swirling above me all day swallowed me up, and I broke. "I'm sorry, Drake. I'm so sorry." Hot, fat tears rolled down my face while I stared at his photo, forever young and perfect. "I hope that wherever you are, you aren't mad. I'll never forget you, ever. But I need to move on with my life. I can't stay stuck in love with you forever. It hurts too much. I think if you were alive, you would have hated Hayden." I laughed without humor. "You couldn't be more different."

I sighed and picked up the picture, pressing a kiss to the glass. "You'll always have a place in my heart, Drake. Even if I eventually make room for someone else. No one could ever replace you." I set it back down on the table and wiped at my eyes, probably smearing my makeup all over my face.

Then something happened. I felt almost at peace for the first time since Drake had died. It was as if the weight of his ghost loosened its grip on me, and all I was left with was a warm feeling in my chest. I took one last look at his picture and smiled to myself before picking up my glass of wine, raising it in toast, and downing the whole thing in one gulp.

I felt lighter, freer. It had been so long since I'd felt that way. Over three months ago, the last time I'd spoken to Drake. I used to sit here and think about how differently I would have done things had I had the ability to go back in time. I wouldn't have waited a whole year to meet him, or I would have asked him to come earlier than he had so he wouldn't have been there to have the accident. Now I was thinking about my future and about how I wanted to pull myself out of my grief and truly live life.

All thanks to meeting Hayden and him showing me there was still so much in life left to enjoy. What a difference a week made.

Resting my head on the back of the couch, I recalled the many conversations I'd had with Drake about life. He'd convinced me I was worth something after so many years of feeling unwanted and unloved by so many foster parents. The only one I felt cared for me at all was Miss Caroline. I picked up my phone to call her. I had something I needed to say, something she deserved to hear.

When I got her voicemail, I said, "Hey, Miss Caroline, it's me, Juliet. I just wanted to tell you, you were right. I'll never forget Drake, but I think I can make room in my life for someone else. Hayden has been really good for me, even in this short amount of time. I feel like I've made more progress just in the time I've known him than I have over the last few months combined. It isn't love or anything close to what I had with Drake, it's too early for that, but it's something different that's made me see there's more to life than how I've been living it. And thank you, for always being there. I don't think I've ever really told you how much you mean to me, but you also hold a special place in my heart. You took a chance on me when not many people would, and it made all the difference. I'm grateful for you and for everything you brought to my life. Anyway, I'll stop being sappy. Give my love to your family. Love you, Miss Caroline." I hung up and clutched the phone to my chest.

I felt excited for life, ready to hop onto the dragon that had been haunting me and slay it until it lay at my feet. The guilt over moving on hadn't pummeled me nearly as bad as I'd thought it would. Morgan had asked me if I was happy, and I realized I was. For the short amount of time I'd have Hayden in my life, I was going to live life fully. And when he was gone, I'd find a way to move on from him, too.

Feeling confident and more sure of myself than I had in a while, I decided to try something I hadn't really ever felt comfortable doing. I went to my room and found my most sexy lingerie. Lying on my bed, I opened the camera on my phone and snapped pictures. With shaking hands, I found the best one, and before I could change my mind, I sent it to Hayden with the caption *just look what you're missing out on.*

I didn't have to wait long for his reply.

You're killing me, babe.

I could hardly believe how brazen I had been to send him that photo. I had only ever sent Drake one sexy picture in the entire year we'd been together, and even then it had taken me months to pluck up the courage to do it.

Deciding I could be even more courageous, I took it one step further and typed a reply.

I guess I'll just have to play alone.

Babe. I would come play, starting with making your delectable ass red for teasing me, if I wasn't caught up.

A heatwave tore through me, my stomach clenching with need. I'd never been spanked before, unless I counted the one time one of my ex's tried to and ended up just smacking my leg, and I didn't count that. I had a feeling with Hayden it would be an experience to remember.

Fuck it. I'll be done here in an hour. Try to stay awake.

Yes, sir.

I left on the lingerie and covered it up with my robe. It felt like I'd touched a live wire, sparks going off inside me in an insanely strong current. He was coming over, and just knowing he was going to be here touching me was enough to send a wet rush between my legs.

I tried waiting patiently on the couch, distracting myself with TV and games on my phone for the next hour. When an hour and a half came and went, I bit at my nails. What if he didn't show up after all? At the two-hour mark, frustration built up inside me, and I shut the TV off. It was nearing ten-thirty, so I went to my bedroom feeling ridiculous. I was just climbing into bed when there was a pounding at my door.

Maybe it was a little petty, but I took my time going to the door. I wanted him to wait like I'd had to. I finally unlocked the door and cracked it open, and he pushed inside and pressed me against the wall with a searing kiss, kicking the door closed. He wasted no time ripping my robe from my body and looking me up and down in my lingerie.

"Fucking Christ," he hoarsely muttered as he peeled them from my body.

Picking me up by my underarms, he pressed me harder into the wall. I wrapped my legs around his waist while he unzipped his pants and shoved them down. In one swift movement, he planted himself deeply inside me and began to move.

Chapter Thirteen

Hayden stayed over that night, holding me the whole time while we slept. I was in an exceptionally good mood the next day, so I barely gave second thought to Carter's gross flirting. I smiled politely and waited for him to go away. If it weren't for me promising to stay late, I'd be asking to leave early so I could drag Hayden to bed. Morgan was right. I had a lot of missed time to make up for in the sex department. But never in my life had sex been so fiery and satisfying.

All through my day I was distracted by the remembrance of our unions. I was bordering on obsessed with the things he did to my body. I wasn't sure I'd ever get enough. I'd worn a skirt today for easier access, that way we didn't have to waste any time once we got back to my place. I had it all mapped out in my head.

At lunch I spilled to Morgan how he'd come by late, and her face lit up with enthusiasm.

"You're one lucky bitch," she'd said.

I knew she was right. I was lucky that I'd found someone willing to take on my baggage and start something with me. We weren't dating or anything as far as I knew, but I liked the arrangement we had. As long as there was enough sex, there wouldn't be time for feelings, and with him inevitably leaving to go back to another country, I couldn't afford to have feelings.

It felt like a hundred degrees in the office, so I went to the thermostat to check the setting. It read eighty-five. I scoffed and lowered it to a reasonable degree and taped a paper to it that read Do Not Touch. Back at my desk, I fanned myself with a folded-up paper as I got back to work. I hoped that if I finished what I was working on early enough I could start on the extra work Carter had for me and get out of there sooner.

He called me into his office toward the end of the day and gave me a rundown on what we'd be working on. I didn't miss that he stared at my breasts and bared legs nearly the whole time. It made me uncomfortable, so I crossed my arms over my chest until he dismissed me.

As everyone began shuffling off, giving me looks of pity, I huffed a deep sigh and moved to the conference room where Carter had set up laptops and the files we had to work on. He'd insisted that we work together, and I didn't care as long as we got done on time. I wanted out of there so I could take Hayden home and show him how much I appreciated him. I had yet to use my mouth on him, but I wanted to. I very much wanted to know what he tasted like, imprint that knowledge in my brain for a long time to come.

"Okay, we have about four files to go through tonight," Carter said as he swept into the room, his massive ego following behind him, taking up the whole room.

We worked quietly together, and I was almost surprised that he managed to stay professional. These files must have been urgent, otherwise I would have expected sideways glances and inappropriate comments all evening.

When I finished up my last file, I rolled my head around to work out the kinks, and Carter moved behind me, massaging my shoulders. "That's okay, Mr. Dunlap. Thanks, though."

"Nonsense, you know I like to take care of my employees. And please, call me Carter."

He continued to massage me, making me more and more

on edge and anxious to get out of there. Not knowing what else to do, I slowly rose and tried to push past him, but he stepped in front of me.

"You're a very beautiful woman, Juliet."

I didn't like where this was heading, so I tried to step around him again, only for him to grab my wrist and jerk me into him. He pressed his lips to mine, and I twisted my face away. He gripped my arm so tight I was afraid it would leave bruises.

"You're hurting me," I cried out, trying to rip my arm away from his grasp.

He put his hand in my hair, gripping tightly, and pushed me down onto the table until I was bent over it. I struggled, but it was no use, he was much stronger than I was.

He ran his hand up the back of my thigh, shoving my skirt up. I choked on a sob in defeat. I knew what was coming and I was helpless to stop it. He ripped my panties down to my knees, the sound of his zipper coming down loud. I waved my arms about, knocking the laptop to the floor.

I cried harder and begged him, "Please don't do this, please. I won't tell anybody, just don't do this. Please!" Everything came out as one jumbled mess, and I fought against the hold he had on me, but he had a death grip on my hair, and nothing I did worked.

"I've wanted you for so long," he practically growled and moved closer into me.

"Help!" I screamed as loudly as I could manage through my tears. "Someone help me!"

"No one can hear you, Juliet. They've all gone home," he gloated.

I just continued to sob into the table. Then his body was lifted off me, his hand coming untangled from my hair in a harsh jerk. I collapsed to the floor. Hayden was on top of Carter, drilling his fist into his face over and over again. I scrambled to my feet and pulled on Hayden's raised fist.

"Stop, you're going to kill him," I shouted in a panicked voice.

"It's what he deserves," Hayden bit out, but he eased off him.

Carter lay in a bloody lump on the floor, clutching his face.

When Hayden turned to me, his eyes were wide and wild, but he gently cupped my face and looked me over. "Babe," he whispered, holding me close and trapping my head against his chest.

I cried so hard my body trembled. When I'd calmed down some, he drew back and reached into his back pocket for his phone.

"What are you doing?" I asked.

"Calling the fucking cops. It's either that or I'll finish him off myself."

My first reaction was to beg him not to, but I scanned through my options quickly. If I didn't, I couldn't continue working here, and if I left, he'd just target someone else. I couldn't let what almost happened to me happen to anyone else, so I nodded weakly. Hayden punched in the number and asked for the police to come as quickly as possible.

I wrapped my arms around myself, trying to process what had just happened. If it hadn't been for me telling Hayden to come up and wait in the office lobby, he'd have never been here to stop Carter. More tears burned in my eyes, and I sniffled.

Hayden stood over Carter, who had moved to a sitting position, watching him. Carter had tried to get up and run off once, but Hayden grabbed his collar and jerked him back down to the floor.

"Don't you fucking move, you piece of shit, or I swear I'll kill you," Hayden threatened.

Carter glared up at him through the one eye that wasn't swollen shut.

"Your boyfriend is quite violent, Juliet," Carter sneered in my direction.

Hayden crouched and got in his face. "You don't talk to her. You don't even look at her. You sit here and shut up until they come haul your ass off. I'm protective of what's mine, and I won't hesitate to choke the life out of you if you don't leave her be."

Hayden smacked the side of Carter's face twice and gave me a long, sad look while I sat huddled in the corner. I could tell he wanted to comfort me, but if he left Carter there unsupervised there was no doubt in my mind that Carter would take off running.

But in that moment, I wasn't focused on what had happened, I was focused on what Hayden had said. He'd called me his. Even with the shock I felt over what had nearly happened to me, my heart still soared over his statement.

The police arrived fifteen minutes later and arrested Carter after taking both mine and Hayden's statements with a promise to be in touch. When the office was empty of everyone but Hayden and me, he crossed to me and wrapped me up in his arms again.

"Let's get out of here, yeah?"

I nodded against his chest, and he took my hand, leading me to the elevator. Once we were in the jeep heading to my apartment, I relaxed a little more. I was safe now with Hayden, and Carter couldn't hurt me anymore. When we stopped in a parking space in front of my building, Hayden helped me down, and we climbed up the flights of stairs to my apartment. I tried and failed to get the key in the lock. I was still quaking from the adrenaline of being violated, so Hayden gently took the key and opened the door.

He led me to the couch, where he settled me into his lap,

and I broke down all over again. I clutched his chest as my tears wet his shirt. Soothingly he rubbed my back and whispered comforting words to me over and over again.

"I'm so sorry, baby. It's going to be okay, I've got you now," he said, and it only made me cry harder.

I couldn't stop thinking about what would have happened if I'd just told him to wait for me outside. Carter would have been successful, and I would have walked away from it completely shattered. Right now, I was only partly broken, and I knew it would take me a while to move past it.

Empty of tears, I sat up in his lap and put my hands on his cheeks, leaning in and kissing him softly. "Thank you," I managed to say through the tightness in my throat. "If you hadn't been there I—" I couldn't even finish my sentence.

"Let's not think about what could have happened. I was there and I stopped it. That's all that matters."

I nodded and laced my fingers through his. I was almost worried that he wouldn't want anything to do with me now that another man had put his hands on me.

"Are you . . . I mean, does it bother you that he touched me?"

"Fuck, yes, it bothers me. It infuriates me. I almost wished I *had* killed him."

"But does it change things between us?"

His head tilted slightly toward his shoulder, and he frowned. "You think I'd just leave you because some asshole saw an opening and tried to take advantage of you?"

I looked down at where our hands were linked, and he squeezed my hand to get my attention. When I glanced back up again his face had grown soft.

"Juliet, I'm a selfish man. I want you all to myself for as long as I can have you. I'd do nearly anything to make that happen. But what someone else decides to do is out of your control. I would never place blame on you for what someone else chose to do to you. This changes nothing between us. I still want you as much as ever, love."

He stroked my cheek with his fingers, and I closed my eyes to the fresh tears that welled up.

"I know you have your issues," he said, "and I'm not going to press you to talk about them. I promise you I might do stupid shit sometimes, but you're the first right thing I've done in a while. I'm not trying to fuck that up, okay?"

"Okay," I whispered back.

"Let's get you to bed."

I climbed off his lap only to have him lift me into his arms, bridal style, and carried me to the bedroom.

"Is it okay if I help you undress?"

"Yes," I answered. I wanted someone else's hands on me, I wanted Hayden's hands on me. I didn't want the last hands to have touched me intimately to be Carter's. So I let Hayden remove my clothes with a gentleness I wouldn't have thought him capable of if I wasn't experiencing it. When I was down to my underwear, Hayden led me to the shower and gently pushed me in under the water once it had heated enough. Moments later he slipped in and wrapped his arms around me. Already I felt safer, but I still didn't feel clean. As if he could read my thoughts, Hayden grabbed the soap and began gliding it over my body, washing away the lingering touches that I was afraid would haunt me forever.

"Better?" he asked after rinsing the soap from my body, and I nodded. Reaching behind me, he shut off the water and got out, returning to wrap me in a towel.

I moved past him into the bedroom and fell onto the bed. I watched him while he toweled me off and tucked me in.

"Are you staying?"

He slid in beside me and wrapped an arm around me. "I'm not leaving you alone after tonight, love. Not unless you tell me to go."

"Never." I wanted him next to me. He was my rock right now, the only thing keeping me from slipping under the waves.

We lay there without speaking for a long time, but neither of us fell asleep. We just stared into each other's eyes, stroking each other all night long wherever there was exposed skin. Nothing needed to be said. Our eyes said it all. His spoke of his relief and happiness to be right there next to me, and I tried to convey all of my appreciation and emotion with mine.

It was sunrise before I knew it, and as the light filtered in through my blinds, I traced my fingertips along Hayden's lips, wanting to remember every nuance of them. I hadn't slept all night and I didn't even feel tired. I was wide awake with fear and relief and the knowledge that I was on borrowed time with Hayden. Every second counted. He kissed my fingertips then, and I looked up into his deep black eyes. I almost wished I hadn't. I realized then how truly screwed I was.

I was screwed because I was starting to feel something for Hayden, and that scared me more than anything had in a long time.

Chapter Fourteen

I called off of work with Hayden's insistence. By then the higher-ups had heard that Carter had been arrested, so I'd had to explain the situation to them to a shameful degree, all while on speakerphone. They gave me the rest of the week and assured me that my job was secure. My worst fears had been alleviated when they'd told me Carter's employment had been permanently terminated. I wouldn't have to see him again unless this whole thing went to court.

Currently I was on the phone with Morgan, who had called at lunch to ask me where I was. I winced when I realized I hadn't even bothered calling to tell her what had happened, but I'd had a long night and all I truly wanted was for Hayden to continue comforting me like he had.

"Holy shit, Juliet, are you going to be okay" she asked once I'd finished telling her what had transpired.

"I think so. I'm better than I was last night at least. The shock is starting to wear off some." I kicked a rock outside Berkley's garage where Hayden had brought me, not wanting to leave me alone but still needing to keep his obligations to his friend. I hadn't walked in yet. Morgan had called me just as we were getting out of the jeep and I didn't want her to worry.

"Do you need anything? I can leave work to come be with you if you need me."

She really was the best friend I could ever have asked for.

"No, it's okay. I'm with Hayden right now, so I'm not alone. But maybe I'll come by later for dinner? We can order takeout and watch crappy movies like we used to."

She agreed, and we said our goodbyes.

I walked in, pulling my coat tighter against me. There was a slight breezy draft blowing into the garage through the bay doors. Most of the snow had already melted, but the chill clung to the air.

"Hey, kiddo, good to see you," Berkley enthused once I'd come close enough to where he and Hayden stood. He pulled me into a hug and gave me a bright smile.

"Kiddo? I'm pretty sure I'm older than you," I pointed out.

"How old are you," he questioned smugly.

"Twenty-five."

"I'm thirty, chickadee."

I widened my eyes. He looked much younger than me, like he'd maybe just turned twenty-one.

"No way, liar."

He pulled out his license for me to examine, and sure enough, he was thirty.

"But we can take comfort in knowing we're both younger than this old man here," he joked as he slapped Hayden on the back.

Hayden rolled his eyes and punched Berkley on the arm.

"Ow, asshole."

"Walk it off, toothpick," Hayden responded.

He wasn't wrong, though. Berkley did resemble a toothpick with a mass of long, stick-straight brown hair. I giggled while the two bickered back and forth, glad I'd decided to come along.

"Knock-knock," a voice called out from the front office.

"Back here," Berkley shouted, and a second later Jade stepped into the bay area. Berkley gave her a quick hug, but Hayden busied himself working on a car that was raised on a platform.

"Hayden, I just wanted to come thank you for coming over the other night," she purred, making sure to stare me down while she said it.

She was trying to stake a claim, but she was either purposely ignoring or totally ignorant of the fact that I was already well on my way to staking my own claim. I glanced at Hayden, who was grimacing. He cast his gaze to me.

"I really needed you, and you came through," she said.

"Just being a good friend, Jade," he replied, rubbing the back of his neck.

"Maybe we can go out for drinks tonight," she suggested.

I stood by quietly, letting this all play out however it was going to. I wasn't usually a jealous person, but Jade gave me a bad feeling, and I knew it was because she was after Hayden.

Hayden glanced at me then said, "I'm busy."

Relief stirred in me, but I tried not to let it show. I wanted to seem as impassive as possible. Berkley was frowning and glancing between Jade and Hayden.

"Maybe tomorrow, then. I owe you for that favor," she said.

What favor was she talking about? Finally, I interjected, "I'm busy tonight, so you should go."

Hayden didn't seem very happy about it. "I—" he began, but Jade cut him off with a squeal.

"Perfect, I'll meet you at the usual bar at nine." She shot me a withering, triumphant smirk then added, "And I guess we'll see where the night takes us."

That was taking it a little too far, so I turned on my heel and walked out to the jeep out of their line of sight. Berkley said something that was muffled by the sound of the wind blowing past my ears, but I didn't want to stay within earshot. Leaning against the jeep, I tried to take deep breaths to calm myself down. I didn't know why I'd suggested he go anywhere with her, I guess mostly to show that I trusted him. But I didn't trust her, so on second thought, it had been a stupid suggestion to make.

Hayden rounded the jeep angrily and stopped in front of me. He hauled me into him and kissed me deeply. I melted against him for a moment but then stepped away.

"I hope you don't seriously believe anything is happening there," he said gruffly.

"What favor is she talking about?"

He sighed and scrubbed a hand across his stubbled chin. "Monday night when I came over late? I was helping her move out of her abusive ex-boyfriend's house while he was working. That's what she was talking about. Berkley was there too, along with Garrett and Adam. You can ask any of them. I never touched her."

"I believe you," I said, truly meaning it.

He seemed surprised at first, as if he wasn't used to anyone believing a word he said. "I'm sorry for the shit she said. She crossed a line, and I need you to know I'm not going anywhere with her tonight. I told her that until she can accept that I'm with you and she is just my friend, then she should steer clear of me."

"You're with me?"

He tilted his head in confusion. "Yes, I thought that's what we were doing here. Am I wrong?"

I smiled at him with a new appreciation. He didn't just want me for my body after all, he wanted *me*. But that didn't bode well for the feelings that were developing. If he went down this road with me, crossing the boundary between lovers and true relationship, my feelings were only going to deepen. That thought terrified me.

"No, I just didn't know. We've never really talked about it, so I wasn't really sure what we were doing, I guess."

He stepped close to me and grabbed my chin in his fingers. "Babe, you think I'd drop everything to be there for just anybody? I checked out of helping Jade move a little early so I could get to you. I spend every free moment I have with you, so yeah, I'd consider this a relationship. I told you I didn't want a fling out of you."

I licked my lips and prepared to have that hard conversation with him that I knew we needed to have. "But you have to go home eventually," I reminded him. "What then?"

"We'll figure it out."

"That's called avoidance, Hayden."

"And I'll avoid thinking about it as long as I can," he quipped.

When Jade walked out of the bay doors into the parking lot, Hayden pulled my face close to his and kissed me. I knew she was watching us. I could feel her glare burning into my back. He continued kissing me long after her car peeled out of the parking lot.

"Hey, lovebirds, she's gone, so you can stop putting on a show. Not everybody wants to see you two with your tongues down each other's throats while you eye-fuck each other."

I broke out into laughter and pushed Hayden away.

For the rest of the afternoon, I watched them both work on one of the cars, Hayden getting dirty with oil. I didn't mind it at all. In fact, it was hot. There was something about his deft hands hard at work that made me squirm around in my chair. When the car finally started up after their fifth test run, Berkley clapped and shouted a relieved, "Hallelujah!"

They did a half handshake, half hug as we left the building and Berkley locked up.

"Thanks for coming to help, man. And bringing eye candy was decent of you, too," he said and winked at me, knowing it would piss Hayden off.

"Watch it," Hayden snarled at him.

Berkley held his hands up in surrender, laughing. I couldn't help but laugh, too.

We hopped into the jeep, and Hayden started the engine. We waved to Berkley when we pulled away, driving back to my place. I was listening to the radio and humming along happily until Hayden spoke.

"What are your plans for tonight?"

"Morgan is coming over. She's worried about me after, you know, last night." I could tell he didn't need the reminder when his mouth turned down and his face twisted in anger all over again.

"Okay, babe. I'll give you girls some time. Berkley mentioned band practice, so I'll probably go watch them play."

I nodded, glad he'd be spending time with his friend, too. We'd been attached at the hip, and while I didn't really mind it, it was also important for us not to neglect the other people in our lives.

He walked me to my door and pressed a kiss to my lips before reluctantly leaving. I dialed Morgan's number to tell her I was home, and she said she was on her way.

She showed up not too long after with a large bottle of wine and a stack of movies. I asked her to play the movie while I got our wine ready, going into the kitchen for a corkscrew. I found myself missing Hayden, though I was glad to spend the evening with Morgan. It had been a while since we'd done this, had a girls' night in.

I returned with the open bottle of wine and two glasses, setting them down onto the coffee table. Morgan took the bottle and poured, filling the glasses far past normal level. I raised a brow, and she shrugged.

"I think we both need it," she said, handing me a full glass before picking up her own and clinking it against mine. "To surviving."

"To surviving," I repeated with a small tilt of my lips.

We took a drink then Morgan turned fully to me on the couch. "How are you doing, really?"

I looked down into my glass of wine sadly. "I'm not good. I'm trying, but sometimes I get these flashes where I remember what it felt like to be helpless, and I can almost still feel his hand in my hair. I don't know if that's going to go away. What if it affects my sex life now? I just got past my previous hang-ups when it came to sleeping with Hayden—I don't need more."

Morgan gave me a sympathetic face and grasped my hand in hers. "It's going to be okay, Juliet, I promise. Hayden really likes you, and he's going to help you through it, I know he will. If he didn't take off before, he isn't going to now."

She gave voice to my fear. I was afraid Hayden would finally see me for the screwed-up woman I was and would decide I wasn't worth it. It was like one bad thing after another continued to happen, and Hayden was a good thing, an anomaly that wasn't meant to happen. I'd had my time with him, but how long could that really last? "You think?"

"I know. I see the way he stares at you. I'd venture as far as to say he's crazy about you. You're the only one doubting it because you aren't paying attention," she pointed out. "You know, after everything you've been through, you deserve someone who looks at you like you're the best thing that ever happened to them. You deserve to find love."

"Whoa, let's not get ahead of ourselves here. We aren't in love or anything. It's been a little over a week. People don't fall in love that fast."

She smirked and rolled her eyes. "Sure they do. It happens all the time."

Morgan didn't believe in love for herself, but she certainly believed in love for other people. I had started to feel *something* for Hayden, but it wasn't love. I would never allow myself to fall in love with someone who lived a world away ever again. He'd told me we'd figure things out when he had to go back home, but I wasn't hopeful. I knew exactly what would happen. We'd try to make things work for a while and we'd talk as much as we could, but eventually we'd both get tired and call it quits.

It had been different with Drake. There was still that anticipation of meeting, but Hayden had already had me. And I'd already had him. When we were no longer physically together, we'd grow frustrated, and it would cause problems. Maybe it was better to end things now before it got out of control.

"I know that look," Morgan said. "What are you thinking about now?"

"Hayden has to go back home to England at some point. Maybe I'm fooling myself by thinking we could ever possibly have anything normal. I think I need to put a nail in it now before it's too late." I reached for my phone, but Morgan got to it first.

"Don't you dare," she screeched. "You find something good for the first time since Drake and you're just going to throw it away because you're scared? I'm not going to let you make this mistake. You're going to regret it if you do."

I watched my friend who had my phone hidden behind her back and a fierce expression on her face. "Give me my phone, Morgan."

Shaking her head emphatically, she said, "Nope. I'm holding your phone hostage until you come to your senses."

As if on cue, my phone rang, and Morgan smiled when she saw who was calling. Hitting the answer button, she put the phone up to her ear and said, "Hello, Hayden. Juliet can't come to the phone until she stops being an idiot." She paused, listening to him speak. "Yes, an idiot."

I gritted my teeth and tried to snatch my phone away

from her, but she was too fast. "Give it back, Morgan," I complained.

"She's doing all right, considering," she answered him, ignoring my pleas. "I'll be gone by ten. She'd love for you to come over." Pause. "Sure, I'll wait with her until you get here. Ta-ta."

She stabbed at the screen to end the call and gave me an innocent smile.

"I'm going to kill you," I shouted at her, and she winked.

"I'm doing you a favor. If you still feel like ending things when you see him face to face, then I'll step back and let you ruin one of the only good things that's happened to you. I won't be happy about it, but if I'm right, and I know I am, you're going to take one look at him and realize how foolish that whole breaking up with him train of thought was. Trust me, I know what I'm talking about." She took a sip of her wine and let me stew.

What if she was right and breaking things off with him wasn't the right decision? I thought maybe it would be easier now rather than later, but I couldn't say for sure. It was going to hurt either way. Now or then, it was going to suck big time to let him go, and I needed to go ahead and prepare myself for when that day came, whenever it came.

I needed to start by guarding my heart. When he was around, rational thought fled me, and I lost myself in him. He was like a brilliant flame, and you know what they say about playing with fire. You always get burned.

Chapter Fifteen

A week passed by quickly, the end of February approaching. I'd kept my job, comforted by the knowledge that Carter would never return and was barred from the property. They'd hired an older woman to take his place, and it was like the entire work environment shifted. None of the women in my office were on edge anymore, everyone silently celebrating Carter's removal.

On Monday as I returned to work, I was worried that everyone would know exactly what had happened, but it seemed the big bosses hadn't let it slip that I was the one involved in his crime. For that I thanked them. I didn't want my coworkers to look at me with pity every day like they had since I'd lost Drake. I just wanted to move on and do my work.

Things with Hayden had been rapidly progressing. We spent every bit of free time we had together when I wasn't with Morgan and he wasn't with Berkley. We cooked dinner together, watched TV together, went on walks around my neighborhood, and he'd even taken me out a couple of times to ride his bike for fun. The week had been full of all things Hayden, and I'd quickly forgotten my plan to break up with him. I had to be a glutton for punishment. I was only delaying the inevitable, but I just told myself I'd deal with it when I was forced to and decided to enjoy being with him while I still could.

I was sitting on a bar stool at the Harbinger with Morgan, waiting for Hayden and Berkley to show up. It was Thursday after work, and I desperately needed a drink. While I was happy we had a woman boss now, she was a stickler for rules and didn't hesitate to add more files to my growing pile. She was the only one who knew what had truly happened and she called me into her office nearly every day to ask me if I needed more time off, because my performance had been suffering.

I just told her I'd try harder and that I didn't want to miss more work. I needed to get back into the swing of things and leave that night with Carter behind in the past. Normal, that was what I needed.

"Juliet, my one true love, good to see you," Berkley drawled, settling in across from Morgan.

Typically, Morgan and I sat at the bar, but we'd grabbed a table this time since we had planned on meeting the guys. It just seemed easier to converse this way than if we'd sat at the bar.

"Berkley," Hayden said gruffly, planting a kiss against my lips in a show of ownership before sitting in front of me.

I chuckled when Hayden shot him a dark look that said, *all mine.* I wasn't normally one for the possessive types, but it was doing things to me this time around. It made me want to pull him under the table and show him just how much I belonged to him in this moment.

We still hadn't slept together since that evening with Carter. It wasn't from my lack of trying. It was almost as if he was afraid I couldn't handle it, but the frustration was wearing on me. We'd taken Morgan's car to the bar. I fully intended on dragging Hayden back to my house and demanding he ravish me all night long. I had a plan and I was going to stick to it.

"Chill, caveman. No need to bang away on your chest in front of me." Berkley snorted as a waitress came by to take drink orders.

I'd already finished my first drink so I ordered another. Morgan kept her glass clutched firmly in her hands, never taking her attention from it for long. That night at Club Rogue had affected her more than she'd let on, and I knew it. But as always, she was stellar at shoving it all down and blazing her way through whatever life dished her. It wasn't healthy, but no amount of psychoanalyzing her would make a difference. Morgan was who she was. Closed off by nature, only letting a select few see her vulnerability. I held it close to my heart that I was one of those people.

"Morgan, this is Berkley, Hayden's best friend. And this is my best friend, Morgan." I introduced the two, and they shook hands across the table.

I had almost hoped there was a spark there, but no luck. They just smiled at one another and started in on a conversation about cars. Morgan's dad was a lifelong mechanic back in Connecticut where she was originally from. She'd moved here for college and liked this mountainous area of North Carolina enough to stay. I'd also like to think that my being here was in part a reason in her decision. We'd been inseparable in college, and not much had changed since.

I slipped my shoe off under the table, gliding my foot up Hayden's leg slowly. He raised an eyebrow at me but pretended nothing was happening. I went higher until it came right between his legs, where I stroked him through his pants. He choked on his sip of beer, slamming the glass on the tabletop. I stifled my laugh by biting down on my bottom lip.

He turned his dark gaze my way, and a flash of heat shone in his eyes. His look said *you're in big trouble,* but I didn't let it deter me. I continued to stroke him, and he grew harder. His hands grasped my ankle and tickled the sole. I burst out laughing, trying to twist it away. Morgan and Berkley glanced over, their conversation coming to a halt, with fixed bafflement on their faces.

"Are you two okay?" Morgan asked, narrowing her eyes between Hayden and me.

"P-perfectly fine," I sputtered, beaming at her.

Hayden looked down, and his cheeks dimpled in that way I loved so much.

"Fucking weirdos," Berkley muttered while he and Morgan smiled at each other.

They both seemed really happy for us, and my heart melted a little. We had good friends, probably the best. And I was happy that I could now call Berkley my friend, too.

"I need the bathroom, coming with?" Morgan's expression told me I didn't have a say in the matter, so I slipped my shoe back on as inconspicuously as I could and followed her toward the back of the bar where the bathrooms were located.

When the door shut behind us, she turned to me and raised an eyebrow. "What are you up to?"

I sighed and leaned against the counter before saying, "It's Hayden. He's barely touched me at all, let alone slept with me, since what happened with Carter. He just treats me like I'm this fragile ornament made of glass and one wrong move could shatter me. It's driving me insane."

"So you decided to feel him up under the table? Don't give me that shocked face, you weren't very secretive about it."

My face flushed, and I shrugged defeated. "What else am I supposed to do to get his attention?"

"Have you tried taking your clothes off and pouncing on him? That's what I'd do," she suggested.

I knew I was neither brave nor bold enough to do something so forward, so I shook my head.

"Look, go home with him tonight. I'll offer to drop Berkley off, and the rest will follow. Trust me."

"I hope you're right," I answered.

We left the bathroom and headed back to the table.

For the next hour the four of us talked, and I continued to shoot glances in Hayden's direction. He'd slide his eyes over to me, his expression unreadable.

"Well, it's getting late. What do you say I drop you off at home Berkley? My car keeps making weird noises, and I could use an expert ear to tell me what's wrong."

"Uh," he began, but one narrowed gaze from Morgan, and his face dawned with understanding. "Right, yes, that would be great. I'll definitely take a look."

We all stood, and I hugged both Morgan and Berkley goodbye, trailing along behind them to the exit. Hayden followed up behind me, his presence so palpable it almost felt like a caress. He helped me into the jeep, and I twisted my fingers together in anticipation. It was true that he hadn't tried to sleep with me once over the past week, but I hadn't exactly reached out on that front either. I didn't know how to take control, but tonight I'd have to if I wanted this to happen.

Quietly, we drove to my apartment, Hayden linking his fingers with mine like he always did. It was the closest he'd come to touching me lately. He hadn't come right out and said that he was drawing away because of what had almost happened to me, but I knew that was the cause. His careful treatment of me had begun right after. I wasn't porcelain, I could handle being with him. In fact, I craved it now even more so. I felt like I had to cleanse myself of Carter's touches. Only Hayden would be able to help me past that. Morgan was there for me, I knew she was, but Hayden could offer me certain things that involved intimacy.

Once in my apartment, we sat on the couch, and I immediately moved over into his lap. His hands came to my hips, holding me in place when I ground my ass into him.

"Babe," he whispered on a grunt.

Deciding it was now or never, I dug deep inside me for the only semblance of courage I had and kissed him, muttering against his lips, "I want you."

"You aren't ready yet," he mumbled back.

"But I am. Please," I begged, running my hands over his sweater, his muscles rippling under my touch.

His control was waning, I just needed to push him a little more. I bit down on his earlobe before saying, "I want you to tie me up."

His breath was coming in fast, labored gasps, and he moved his hands from my hips to my lower back, pressing my body into his.

"Please be sure about this, love," he rasped as he stood, still holding me against him.

"I'm one hundred percent sure," I assured him.

Without further argument, he walked us to the bedroom, taking my mouth with his feverishly.

My heart pounded painfully, all the desire I possessed building up in me, close to ripping me to shreds. He broke the kiss, tossing me onto the bed and gripping the bottom of my sweater, lifting it over my head and throwing it behind him. He ripped my bra from my body, then glanced around in search of something. He crossed the room to my robe and pulled the sash from it, returning to me. Gently grabbing my wrists, he tied them together in a perfect knot. I tested the restraint, and it held fast.

"Is this what you want?" he asked, his voice barely above a whisper.

"Yes," I answered, my own voice trembling with want.

Without another word he unbuttoned my slacks and slipped them down my legs along with my panties. I lay there naked and restrained, wholly vulnerable, but I'd never felt so strong in my life. I'd asked for what I wanted, and I was getting it. There was a certain power in that that gave me strength.

I watched him slowly peel his clothes from his body, gracing me with the view of his tanned, sculpted perfection. He moved toward me, a feline grace as he prowled then knelt at my feet. Kissing the tops of them, he created a path with his mouth all the way up my body, ignoring all the places I needed him. I wriggled around, trying to catch his lips, but he pulled back until I went still every time.

"I'm in charge here, love. I'll give you what you want, but I want to hear you beg for it."

I gulped. What had I gotten myself into? "Please," I squeaked out.

"Please what?" His eyes were alight with excitement. He was thoroughly enjoying this, torturing me.

He traced a finger around one of my nipples, and it pebbled painfully.

"Please, touch me."

"Where do you want me to touch you, Juliet?" He wanted me to spell it out, tell him word for word what I wanted, what I needed.

"Touch my breasts. Please," I continued to beg.

The dampness between my legs grew, and a flood of wet desire pooled within me. He stopped tracing along my chest with his finger and grasped my nipple between his thumb and pointer, pinching it delicately. I raised my hips off the bed against his body, his hard length pressing into my skin.

"So responsive." His mouth wrapped around my other nipple while he continued to tweak the one between his fingers.

A strangled sound gripped my throat and spilled out when I tried to delve my tied-together hands into his hair. With his free hand he pushed mine back over my head.

"Keep them there, or I'll tie them to the bed," he warned.

An urgency sped through me, and I envisioned his strong hands working to bond me to the headboard.

"Don't make promises you won't keep," I challenged him, surprising even myself.

Before I had the chance to blush, he chuckled darkly and said, "You *want* me to, don't you?"

I nodded sheepishly. He climbed off me, looking around the room before digging through my drawers. He found two scarves and made his way back over to me. Untying the silk sash from around my wrists, he separately tied them to either post on my bed. I felt even more vulnerable, unable to move my arms more than a fraction of an inch to either side.

He stood back to admire his handiwork and sucked his bottom lip in between his teeth. His gaze roamed my body as I laid there splayed naked across the bed.

"Never have I seen something so fucking beautiful," he ground out. "Need you now. Fuck."

"What's wrong" I asked, hoping he wasn't about to change his mind.

"I don't have any condoms with me. Didn't think I'd need them tonight." He rubbed his hand down his face, obviously kicking himself for not being prepared.

"I'm on birth control, if that makes a difference," I informed him. I'd been on birth control since I was old enough to get it without parental permission. You could never be too careful. And I trusted him. I didn't think anything bad would happen if we went sans condom for one night.

He nodded and came over me, kissing my lips fervently. He barely grazed my opening with the head of his cock, and I strained with my hips to push myself down onto him. When he bent his head to suck my throat, he entered me, one hard, long thrust that had me gasping. Biting into that sensitive spot where my neck and shoulder connected, he withdrew and flexed his hips, thrusting into me again.

"Hayden," I breathed.

"Love being inside you, Juliet," he mumbled against my throat, still sucking and biting at my skin.

I was muttering incoherent words of encouragement, prodding him to keep going, not wanting this to ever end. I tested the restraints, loving how it felt to be bound and there for him to do with as he pleased as much as I wanted to roam his body with my hands. I longed to sink my nails into his back and run my fingers through his hair. He captured my mouth with his and angled my hips higher, thrusting deeper inside me.

"Oh God," I moaned, my insides clenching.

His fingers dug into my thighs in a bruising way I'd be feeling later while he moved inside me, unrelenting. I was drawing closer, my orgasm hovering just out of reach. I was jumping for it, begging it to come to me, and it did. I came, pulsing around him, tears prickling my eyes. I trembled and quaked, a hard shiver racking my body. I'd never come so hard in my life, the strength of my orgasm thickening my throat with emotion.

Hayden rested his forehead on mine and stilled, releasing himself inside me. His shuddering breath blew across my cheeks. His body shook over me, our harsh breaths mingling together between us. He was in no hurry to leave me, staying connected to me a while longer, and a tear rolled down the side of my face.

He leaned back and gave me a panicked look. "Fuck, did I hurt you?"

"N-No, it's not that. I'm fine. I don't know why I'm crying," I breathed out a short laugh.

He knelt, pulling out, and untied my hands as quickly as he could. When they were free, he scooped me up into his arms and held me close, burying his face in my neck.

"You'd tell me if I did, right?"

I nodded against his shoulder, afraid my voice would catch and break if I tried saying anything at all.

We stayed that way for a long time, embracing one another in the center of my bed, until I pushed against his chest.

"I need to go to the bathroom. Clean up," I explained, and he hesitated before finally letting me go. I climbed off the bed and disappeared into the bathroom, closing the door behind me. After I was finished, I stared at myself in the mirror. My makeup had run, and my hair was wild and untamed. I spent a few seconds cleaning my face and finger-combing my curls enough to settle them back down.

When I opened the door, Hayden was sitting on the side of the bed, his head in his hands. I settled in on the floor in front of him and cupped his face so he'd have to look at me. His expression was tortured, as if he'd done something wrong.

"You didn't hurt me, Hayden," I assured him. "I just . . . I've never experienced something like that, and I guess it just made me a little emotional." My face burned with my confession.

He regarded me strangely, then the corner of his mouth lifted.

"That's what happened?"

I nodded, and he blew out a breath.

"Thank fuck."

"That doesn't weird you out, does it?" I was a little worried it would be too much for him. We'd known each other for a few weeks. It was too soon for anything emotional, yet here I was, crying after sex like some kind of idiot struck dumb by love. I wouldn't even blame him if he ran away at this point.

"Weird me out? On the contrary, I like that you're comfortable enough with me to let yourself go."

The relief I felt was so immense I had to blink away more

tears. "That's never happened before," I admitted when he held me in his lap, kissing the side of my head.

"Never?"

I shook my head. Sex up to this point had been very mediocre. No one I'd been in bed with had ever evoked so many feelings in me just from their touch alone. Many nights I'd fall asleep frustrated when a boyfriend hadn't even tried to make sure I'd come too. But Hayden—he not only made me come harder than I'd ever thought possible, but he took care of me after. His touch was deliberate and gentle, exactly what I needed.

"I haven't had much luck in the sex department, as it turns out," I confided in him. "But I hadn't really realized just how bad it was until now."

"You deserve better than awful sex, love. Glad to do my part."

I snorted at his arrogance, remembering who I was talking to.

"I'm guessing you need to sleep," he said. "It's getting pretty late."

I stifled a yawn and wrapped my arms around his neck. He moved us, sliding under the covers and yanking them up to our necks. I brushed my hand through his hair, searching his face for any panic, but I didn't see anything remotely close to it. Instead, warmth and tenderness reflected back at me.

"Go to sleep, Juliet," he murmured, nuzzling my neck.

My body was tired, full-on exhausted from the life-altering sex we'd just had. I wanted to stand on the top of the highest building in town and scream from the rooftops my joy and contentment. But as usual, my brain thought of all the ways this was going to go wrong. Like when he left. It was impossible not to think of that day because it would come in less than a month and a half, and that didn't feel like enough time with him.

"I can't." I continued raking my gaze across his face, trying to commit every last detail to memory. One day I wouldn't have him here with me.

"Try. I'm here and I'm not going anywhere, so you can stop looking at me like I'm going to vanish if you take your eyes off me."

He'd caught me. Was I really so easy to read?

I snuggled into him, laying my head on his chest, and fell asleep to the steady thump of his heartbeat.

Chapter Sixteen

It was Sunday afternoon, and I was out shopping with Morgan. Things in the bedroom had picked up again, and I wanted to buy something new and sexy to wear for Hayden. With Morgan's expertise, I picked out a baby-blue bra and panty set that pushed my boobs up and made my ass look great. I couldn't wait until I saw him again so I could surprise him. I was already picturing his face as he undressed me, unwrapping me like a gift, to find the new lingerie that I'd bought specifically with him in mind.

Normally we spent weekend evenings together, staying up late discovering each other's bodies, but he was busy with Berkley tonight. Doing what, I didn't know. He'd had been very vague about it. There was a moment when I'd wondered if Jade was involved, but I'd quickly pushed that thought aside. He wouldn't hide it from me if she was going to be there. Surprisingly, for the kind of person Hayden was, he was very open about nearly everything with me.

Today was one of the days where I thought of Drake more than usual, though. Those days were becoming fewer and fewer, that darkness that used to hang over my head every day after I lost him slowly dissipating. I actually managed to go days without pining over the loss of what I could have had with him now. Occasionally I felt a twist of guilt because I was fully moving on now. The people I trusted most were right about never forgetting him. I could never leave him behind in my heart, but I could make room for someone else in my life now. I was breathing easier, not encumbered by so much grief that I could barely get through the day anymore.

"What do you think of this dress?"

I glanced up when Morgan spoke, broken from my train of thought, and she held up a slinky red dress.

"It would look great on you," I answered with a smile.

"I'm totally buying it."

"I know you, you don't buy new dresses unless you're trying to get someone's attention. What gives? I thought you were giving up on men."

She smirked as we made our way to the register.

"Mark has been sniffing around again, and I want to show him what he'll be missing for the rest of his life."

I couldn't help but snicker. Mark had been a fool to let her go in the first place. I guess he didn't find what he'd been searching for in Shannon and realized Morgan was everything he'd been wanting. His loss.

"You're evil, and I love it."

We left the shop with the intention of getting lunch when it started to rain. We ran through the freezing drops back to my car, laughing the entire way. We both looked like drowned sewer rats, her long blonde hair lying flat against her face and my dark curls frizzing up and sticking out in all directions.

"I guess that's it for shopping," Morgan grumbled unhappily. "I still hadn't found the perfect shoes yet."

"We'll find you some shoes soon," I promised and drove away from the boutiques. "Where do you want to go for lunch?"

"Anywhere at this point. I'm starving."

I searched around while we drove and found myself pulling up at Rosa's, the diner Hayden had taken me to.

"What's this place?" she asked.

"They have really good burgers, and I could stand to add

a little grease to my life right now," I explained.

"Sign me the fuck up," Morgan chirped.

We stepped from the car and rushed inside.

It was warm in the diner, much to my relief. I felt soaked to the bone, and a deep chill had set in.

"So, what are you and Lover Boy up to tonight?"

I'd gotten used to Morgan's nicknames for Hayden so I mostly ignored them now. "He's busy with Berkley, so I'm thinking of just having a quiet night at home in front of the TV."

"Want me to stay with you?"

"No, it's fine. I think I'd enjoy some time alone for a change. It's been a while since I've been on my own, and I probably need it. Everyone—you, Hayden, even Berkley—have been a nice distraction, but I eventually need to sit alone and face my demons at some point."

She nodded solemnly, understanding. "I'm just glad you're doing better than you were. I think Hayden has been really good for you, Juliet. I just wish you'd found him sooner. It wasn't easy seeing you so broken up over Drake."

"I still think about him," I said, losing myself in my inner thoughts from earlier. "It's getting easier, though, every day."

"That's really good." She smiled. When our burgers came and she took a bite, she moaned. "This is the best burger I've ever had."

"I told you."

By the time we finished lunch the rain had let up, but dark clouds still hovered around in the distance, telling us that the rain was far from over for the day. We went to a few more shops trying to find the perfect shoes for Morgan's new dress. I might have also bought some tall black pumps to wear with my lingerie.

When it started getting dark out, I drove Morgan home,

watching her struggle up the porch steps with her shopping bags. On my way back to my apartment I sang along to the radio, a sappy love song that I would have sneered at not too long ago. I was happy, full of life, and having better sex than I'd ever thought possible. Everything felt like it was falling into place, even if one day I'd have to give some of it up.

Letting myself into my apartment, I changed into some comfy shorts and a camisole, crashed in front of the TV, and watched reruns of my favorite show.

I must have fallen asleep at some point during an episode. A harsh pounding woke me, and I groggily opened my eyes when the pounding continued. Someone was beating down my door. I pulled myself up off the couch and went to look through the peephole. Berkley stood there with Hayden hanging off him. I immediately rushed to unlock and open the door.

"What the hell?" I asked when Hayden spit blood onto the concrete landing.

"H said you were a nurse. Care to patch up your dumbass boyfriend?" Berkley asked without a hint of panic. In fact, he almost seemed amused, and I didn't find this situation funny even a little bit.

"I went to nursing school, but I never actually practiced. I'm probably a little rusty," I admitted, stepping aside to let them in.

Berkley shoved Hayden onto the couch and sat next to him. Hayden grunted, shifting to get more comfortable. I went into the bathroom to look for my first-aid kit, which was admittedly a little sparse, and returned to the living room.

"Took me forever to get him to tell me where you lived," Berkley rambled on. "He was hell-bent on keeping this from you, but I told him he was an idiot."

"What exactly happened?" I tried keeping my voice calm

as I opened the kit and pulled out some alcohol wipes and bandages.

"Nothing," Hayden groaned, but Berkley talked over him.

"Cage fighting. You think he looks bad? You should see the other guy. Hayden actually won," Berkley scoffed. "Don't know how the bastard managed to stay on his feet, but I'll hand it to him."

I opened my mouth in surprise. I'd thought he'd given that up a long time ago, but I was clearly mistaken. A surge of anger stabbed at me. He could have been seriously injured, worse than he already was.

I tore open an alcohol wipe and smeared it across his busted lip.

"Ouch, goddammit." He winced.

"It's just an alcohol wipe, you big baby. After taking a beating like you did, this should be the easy part," I snapped.

Berkley snickered but stopped when I shot him a dark glare.

"You're mad, aren't you?" Couldn't get anything past Hayden.

"I'm not mad. I'm furious." I dabbed at his lip again, ignoring his scowl.

"Babe, it's not a big deal. I'll be fine by tomorrow."

That wasn't the point, and he knew it. But I ignored him and just focused on cleaning him up. His lip was swollen and bleeding, his right eye was black and nearly closed shut, and a trickle of blood was coming from his nose. There was hardly a place on his face untouched. I could feel him staring at me, though I avoided his eyes altogether as I worked.

It was hard for me to imagine him using his fists to purposely hurt someone. The same hands that held me tenderly, touched me so gingerly. He'd punched Carter, but that was different. That was in my defense. This time he had fought someone for fun? Money? I didn't know why, and I didn't care. He shouldn't have done something so stupid.

"Well, I'm going to go. You two clearly have a lot to talk about, and I don't particularly want to be here for that conversation," Berkley announced, standing to leave.

I was so mad that I didn't want Hayden staying here tonight. I wanted to fix him up and I wanted him to get out so he could think about what he'd done. But Berkley was right. We had a lot to talk about.

"Bye, Berkley," I called after him.

He patted my shoulder and left.

With us two now alone, the walls felt like they were closing in on me. My rage just festered, and when I patched a bandage over a cut on Hayden's cheek and sat back, I knew that rage was going nowhere for a while.

I lifted his shirt, checking him over for any signs of internal damage, and aside from some bruising, he seemed fine other than the mess the other guy had made of his face. I sighed and stood from the coffee table, taking the first-aid kit back to the bathroom. When I turned around, Hayden was standing in the doorway, arms crossed over his chest. I pushed past him to head to the kitchen. I pulled out a bottle of whiskey and threw back a glass, pouring another.

"Are you just going to ignore me all night?" he asked.

"That was the plan, yes."

"For fuck's sake, Juliet," he muttered. "Morgan wasn't kidding about you being impossible when you're angry."

"Tell me why. Why would you do something so idiotic as to get your ass kicked? And what for? Money certainly isn't worth it, and if this is something you do for fun, then we have different definitions of the word fun. Just explain it to me, Hayden. I can't figure out what would possess you to do it." When he didn't say anything, I threw my hands up in the air. "You can sleep on the damn couch tonight."

I left the whiskey on the counter and went to move past him when he caught me by my waist and dragged me back into his chest.

"Don't be mad at me, love. I owed a friend. Told him I'd fight in his place tonight to win his money back for him and that's it. End of story."

"What kind of friend lets you take a beating for them?" I huffed angrily, trying to escape his grasp.

"The kind who's also taken a beating for me."

I didn't even want to know.

"I wasn't going to show up here tonight, but Berkley convinced me to. I can see now that I shouldn't have bothered you."

"So you would have rather *lied* to me? Is that what you're saying? I don't take very well to being lied to." I struggled harder, but it was no use. He wasn't going to let me go until we'd finished talking, so I relaxed against him.

"No, dammit, you're twisting my words around. I just . . . I shouldn't have shown up like this in the middle of the night, and Berkley should have just kept his damn mouth shut instead of springing everything on you the way he did."

"Don't blame Berkley for being honest with me. At least one of you had the balls to tell the truth."

His arm tightened around me. "I'm sorry, okay? I won't do it again," he purred into my ear.

An involuntary shiver raced down my spine. Angry or not, I still wanted the man.

"You'd better not, or I'm not going to talk to you ever again," I muttered sullenly.

"Noted. Now can we go to bed? I want to hold your body to mine. I have a feeling that'll make me feel better."

I should have just made him sleep on the couch like I'd threatened, but I didn't. I let him lead me to the bedroom, and I climbed in as he undressed. His ribs weren't broken, but they were bruised pretty badly, dark shadows beginning to form on his side, prominent in the light of the moon cast in through my window.

When he crawled in next to me with a pained groan and pulled me into his side, I sighed in contentment. My anger was dissipating some, but I couldn't let it go completely. I wasn't just going to forgive him for doing something dumb just because he whispered nice words in my ear and held me close. I wasn't that weak.

I flipped over so I was facing him and searched his battered face for the answers to all the questions I hadn't asked him. The overwhelming desire to kiss his wounds away came over me, but I held back.

"What's on your mind, love?" Hayden questioned me, brushing my cheek with his fingertips.

"A lot," I answered vaguely.

He smirked, his bottom lip cracking open again slightly. "Which I assume you aren't going to talk to me about."

"Not right now I'm not," I confirmed.

He seemed to accept my answer and laid his good cheek across the top of my head.

"Goodnight, Juliet."

"Goodnight, Hayden."

Chapter Seventeen

By the following Tuesday Hayden's face looked much better, and he'd been putting extra emphasis on letting me know where he was going when he was with Berkley, though I hadn't asked. I wanted to trust him to make the right choices and I wanted to never have him banging on my door again in the middle of the night because he'd been beaten to a pulp.

It was March now, one month closer to Hayden's departure. Every day I tried not to think about it, but it snuck up on me when I was sitting reading a book or playing on my phone to pass the time. It seemed to hurt the most when I was with him, though. After we'd slept together, I'd look at him sleeping peacefully next to me and wonder how I was going to get through it knowing he wouldn't be around anymore.

During those times I wondered why I'd done this to myself in the first place. Getting involved with someone who wouldn't be around anymore was a big mistake. It would be like losing Drake all over again, only I'd know Hayden was out there in the world somewhere, probably crawling into someone else's bed. And I didn't like thinking about that a bit.

I didn't have any hope that there was anything we could do to fix the situation. He'd leave, and we'd both be better off trying to move on with our lives. It hurt like hell, but I'd resigned myself to it. At times I thought he sensed me trying to distance myself, and it was those times that he held on even tighter.

I held myself back so hard, but my feelings just kept growing and I knew if I didn't put a damper on it, I'd end up falling in love with him. For all his faults, Hayden was good to me and loyal to a fault. That was hard to find these days. So hard to find that I wanted to cling to him like a barnacle. But I did the exact opposite. It was the smart thing to do and I prided myself on being logical in most situations.

We'd been sitting down to dinner last night when he'd asked me, "What's going on with you, Juliet? You're acting strangely."

"I'm not acting strangely," I'd said.

"You are, though, and I know something isn't right. When you don't want me to cuddle you at night, something is definitely fucking wrong."

I'd gotten up from the table and hid in the bathroom for an hour crying my eyes out. When he'd finally managed to coax me out I'd distracted him from asking more questions by jumping him, kissing him, and dragging him to bed. But it was afterward when he'd started asking questions again that I realized I had nowhere to turn to get out of answering him. I couldn't very well tell him, "Yeah, so I think I have feelings for you, which is stupid because you're going back to London next month, so I'm pulling away to save face." So instead I'd told him that I was just tired from work. How our new boss, Ms. Fisher, was a tyrant who piled on more work than was humanly possible to finish, and I barely had the energy to remember to breathe and blink.

I knew he hadn't believed me, it was clear by the way his endless eyes had narrowed when he'd looked at me. He'd sighed, very audibly I might add, and kissed my temple. He didn't press the issue any further that night, so I'd rolled over and fell asleep.

Currently I was waiting on him to pick me up from work,

sitting on a bench right outside my office building. I was scrolling through my social media apps to pass the time.

"You ruined my life," a voice called out, sounding pained.

I peered up to see what the commotion was about. Carter Dunlap stood not even ten feet away from me. I slowly rose and was starting to back away when he pulled out a gun and pointed it right at me, square in the chest. My legs almost buckled beneath me, and I searched around for anyone who might be able to help me. The only people were on the other side of the street, totally oblivious to what was happening. I opened my mouth to scream, and Carter cocked the gun.

"If you try to call for help, I'll shoot you right now."

I turned back to him. Wild desolation was splayed clearly across his face. I'd gotten a restraining order against him, but a piece of paper did nothing in the face of a crazed man who had lost everything he'd worked for. He had nothing left to lose, and we both knew it.

"Carter—" I began, but he cut me off.

"Shut up! You don't get to speak. I'm going to enjoy watching the life leave your eyes when I kill you," he sneered.

Tears welled in my eyes, because I knew there was nothing I could do. He was going to shoot me, and I was helpless. I had nothing to fight back with, no way to get help unless someone happened upon us. It would be the perfect time for Hayden to arrive, but I also hoped he didn't. I knew he'd end up getting hurt if he did.

I squeezed my eyes shut, waiting for the bullet to discharge from the gun and enter my body, but nothing happened. I opened my eyes again. Carter had the gun to his own head. Panicking, I rushed toward him to stop him from pulling the trigger, and he turned the gun to me and fired.

It was as if it all happened in slow motion.

A searing pain moved through my abdomen, and I went

down to my knees, clutching my torso. I glanced up at Carter, who stood over me with a wicked, evil grin, and my vision blurred. I vaguely remembered hearing someone yelling, and then I remembered nothing at all.

A steady beep and muffled sniffles filtered into my mind, and someone held my hand, squeezing tightly. There was nothing but blackness. I couldn't seem to open my eyes, but I could hear everything.

"Please wake up, love." Hayden. "There's so much I didn't tell you that I should have. I don't want you to go. Not like this." His voice broke.

A lump rose in my throat. I wanted to scream, "I'm okay, I'm awake," but I couldn't make my lips move, couldn't conjure up a single groan or whisper.

My body felt numb except for the biting, sharp pain that stretched across my middle. It hurt so badly that I was sure I was dying. If this was death, I was glad I got to hear Hayden's voice one last time.

Feeling drained just from the few short moments of consciousness, I slipped away again.

My eyes fluttered briefly before I whimpered against the pain that seemed to reign supreme over all else. I tried cracking my eyes open, but the harsh light made me snap them shut once more.

"Juliet?"

I turned my head to the side where the voice had come from.

"Can I get a nurse in here, please?" the same voice called out.

My hand was scooped up, a kiss pressed against the back of it.

"Is everything all right?" a soft voice asked.

"I think she's waking up."

One of my eyes was pried open, and I winced from the blinding light.

"Turn the lights down if you don't mind."

The room darkened some, and I relaxed.

"Miss Banks, can you hear me? My name is Rhonda. I'm a nurse here at St. Clarence's."

A nurse? The hospital. I was in the hospital. It all came flooding back. Carter. The gun. Him shooting me on the sidewalk. I cracked my eyes open in the now dim lighting and let them refocus before my gaze roamed, taking in the room. A kind-faced older woman who reminded me a lot of my mom with blonde hair pulled back into a low bun stood over me to my right.

And so did Hayden to my left.

He was haggard, as if he hadn't slept in centuries. His normal stubble had grown out some, and deep circles lined the skin beneath his eyes. But it was his actual eyes that got me. They were as dark as they'd ever been, and they were tortured.

"Sweetheart," Rhonda said to get my attention, "I need to ask you some questions, okay?"

I nodded and swallowed hard against the thick dryness of my mouth.

"What's your name?"

Easy enough. "Juliet Banks," I croaked.

"Your birthdate?"

"October fifteenth."

"What street do you live on?"

"Orchard Lane."

"What day was it when you were hurt?"

"Um, March fifth, I think."

She nodded as she continued to mark on her paper.

"Is it not still March fifth?" I asked.

Rhonda and Hayden shared a look that did nothing to settle my nerves. I tried sitting up in bed, but my arms slipped out from under me weakly.

"Relax for now. We'll help you get up in just a bit," the kind nurse cooed.

"What day is it?" I snapped, snatching my arm from her gentle grasp.

Hayden cleared his throat and answered so the nurse wouldn't have to. "It's Monday, March eleventh."

Six days. I'd lost six whole days.

"The good news is, the bullet didn't hit anything that would have required immediate surgery," Rhonda said. "Your doctors ran tests, and we've been keeping a close eye on you, and everything seems perfectly normal. If you're up and walking by tonight, we'll see about discharge tomorrow if you're lucky. The doctors may want to keep you around for another night of observation since you've been out so long."

I scoffed. "Perfectly normal? How is any of this perfectly normal?" I was being a brat, but I was scared. Still, I shouldn't take it out on someone who was being kind to me. I shook my head to clear away some of the fog and said, "I'm sorry. It's not your fault."

She patted my arm. "It's okay, dear. You've been through a lot. I'll notify the doctor that you're awake, and he should be in to see you soon. If you need anything, just press the button on the side of the bed that says nurse."

She left the room, and I sighed, but it hurt.

"I want to sit up. I feel stupid just lying here," I complained.

"Let me go ask the nurse if that's okay."

Hayden left to find the nurse, so I stared at the pock-marked ceiling counting tiles. I only got to five before he came back.

"She said you can incline about forty-five degrees."

He pressed a button on the side of the bed until he hit the forty-five-degree mark. I still didn't feel like I was sitting up enough, but it was better than lying flat, so I didn't say anything. What I wanted more than anything was some water. My mouth felt fuzzy and dry. So, so dry.

"Do you have anything to drink?"

He immediately turned and opened a half-empty bottle of water on the table next to the lone chair, then passed it to me.

I drained it within seconds. It helped, but it wasn't enough. I didn't want to seem needy, so I didn't bother asking for more, though I knew he would have gotten it for me.

I knew what I was doing. I was delaying the inevitable talk about what had happened. There was no way I wanted to relive that bit of nightmare over again anytime soon, but I knew I'd have to. Probably many times. What was one more time?

So I sat there quietly and waited for the questions I knew were burning him alive.

"Are you feeling okay?" he finally asked, his voice calm and steady.

I shrugged. "I feel like I've been shot, if that's what you're asking."

He flinched, and I cursed myself for being so insensitive. I sure chose a perfect time in life to live without a filter.

I breathed in through my nose then said, "I'm above the dirt, so I'm doing better than I thought I was. I thought for sure I was going to die."

"I thought you were, too," he quietly admitted.

So much pain in his voice, but hope, too, as if he'd already resigned himself to losing me and it turned out to be a nice surprise that I'd lived after all.

"You were in the ICU for a while, and they wouldn't let

me see you since I wasn't immediate family. You were all alone back there, and I—" He stopped talking for a few seconds. "I'm just so glad you're awake and talking. I didn't like seeing you lying there unmoving. And they couldn't even estimate when you'd wake up. It was hell, Juliet."

My throat tightened as I stared at him. He was barely holding himself together, and I wanted nothing more than to take him into my arms. He still had a faint bruising around his eye, but it was easy to miss if you weren't searching for it, and his lip had healed up nicely. I'd been knocked out for six days while he was recovering from having the hell beat out of him. I wouldn't blame him if he curled up on the floor in the fetal position about right now.

"How long have you been here?" I asked suspiciously.

He didn't look so good.

His eyes met mine again when he answered, "I haven't left since they put you in this room. So I guess . . . four days."

I was about to chastise him and tell him to go home immediately when a choked sob came from the doorway. I glanced over. Morgan and Berkley strolled in. Morgan was crying as she made her way to me and kissed my cheek.

"You're awake," she wailed.

My chin trembled, and I bit back my own tears. In the end I failed and ended up crying along with her. Hayden had taken my hand in his and squeezed. Berkley gave me a warm smile that I returned just as brightly.

"Hayden and I are going to go get you some food. We'll leave you two alone for a minute."

I could tell he wanted to do anything but leave my side, but Berkley must have convinced him. I nodded, and the warmth left me when his hand slipped from mine.

When the guys disappeared from the room, Morgan dabbed at her eyes with a tissue and fanned her face. It was so rare for her to show emotions in front of so many people like this that I was in shock more than anything. It was a true testament to how much she liked Hayden and Berkley.

"You scared the shit out of me, Juliet." She glanced toward the door to make sure Hayden and Berkley were truly gone before she turned to me again. "You know, he hasn't left here since you were allowed visitors. We tried to make him go home and rest, but he said if you woke up he wanted to be here for it."

He'd said as much, but it still felt good to hear it again. It was nice knowing I hadn't been lying here alone the whole time, even though I wished Hayden had been taking care of himself better.

"You know," she continued, "I'm pretty sure that guy is in love with you."

I stared at her wide-eyed, and my pulse jumped erratically. I wasn't sure I'd heard her correctly, so I asked her to repeat herself.

"He's totally in love with you. You don't sit up day and night for days on end by someone's bedside if you don't love them." She beamed at me and sighed wistfully. "You're one lucky woman. I wonder if he has any friends. Other than Berkley, of course."

It turned out that she and Berkley had become fast friends, bonding over cars and music. They'd been coming in together to bring Hayden changes of clothes, food, and toiletries over the last few days, taking care of him while he watched over me. I had almost hoped something would blossom between them, but she made a face when I suggested it.

"He's like an annoying older brother." She laughed. "No way in Hell or any other realm of existence is that happening. May God strike me down if it does."

"You're such a drama queen," I joked, but she nodded her

agreement. She knew she was and she owned it. I wouldn't take her any other way.

"So?" she prompted.

"So, what?"

"So, do you love him, too?"

I was saved from having to answer her by the guys entering the room once more with a bag of assorted foods from the cafeteria. Hayden handed me a large Styrofoam cup of iced water that I greedily sucked down. I wasn't really in the mood to eat, honestly, but I took a few bites of some pudding and a few French fries. I could feel Hayden's eyes on me the whole time, but I tried pretending I didn't notice, scared I'd see in his eyes that he really did love me.

To be totally blunt, I was scared shitless. I didn't want him to love me. That meant there'd be nothing stopping me from pushing my feelings to the side. It was easier if he didn't love me. Then I could convince myself I didn't love him either. And with him leaving in what would now be about three weeks, there was no room for love. He was going to leave me, and I refused to be heartbroken over it.

When the doctor arrived, Morgan and Berkley gave me hugs and left. The doctor explained that nothing important had been punctured, that I'd been very lucky indeed. The bullet went through some muscle and tissue, so I had a few weeks of recovery ahead of me, but with a strict regimen of rest and antibiotics, I'd probably feel better by the end of the week. And he told me that if the nurses thought I could get around well enough without being a fall risk then I could go home tomorrow morning. I wanted out of here so badly.

When he left, the nurse came to help me from the bed, taking my IV pole along with us, and we walked up and down the hallway as Hayden followed along behind us.

"You have a pretty exceptional man back there, you know," she told me with a smile.

I knew my face turned as red as my favorite wine.

"Yeah, yeah I do," I answered, my lips tilting up at the corners.

Deciding I was well enough to go home, the nurse led me back to my room and said she'd put in for my discharge for the morning.

I scooted over on the bed and patted the space beside me for Hayden to lie next to me.

"I don't want to hurt you," he worriedly stated.

"Just get in the damn bed," I demanded.

He eased onto it and wrapped an arm around me, and I settled in against him. Since waking, I had pictured Carter's horrid face as he'd stood over me after shooting me. I'd been sure I'd never see Hayden or Morgan or Berkley ever again, but here I was living and breathing.

"You know the cops are going to come by before you leave for a statement," he informed me cautiously.

I had expected it, but I didn't want the reminder. "Yeah, I figured so. Did they catch him at least?"

"Oh yeah, I knocked that motherfucker out cold. He was still limp when they got there."

Good. It was the very least he deserved.

"I'm so glad I got there in time," he said. "If I'd been a minute later—" He let the words drop off, seemingly afraid of even giving a voice to them.

"Let's not worry about the could haves. I'm alive and I'll be totally fine in a few weeks."

He nodded but was a million miles away, deep in thought.

"Juliet, there's something I need to say and I should have said it long before now."

When he peered down at me, my heart raced.

"I lo—"

I cut him off with a kiss, not wanting him to say the

words out loud. That would make it real, and he couldn't take the words back if he spoke them. When I pulled away his brow furrowed.

"I'm so tired, aren't you tired?" It was a bold-faced lie. I'd slept for six full days and I was wide awake. But I couldn't let this conversation continue.

Hayden sighed and ran his fingers through my hair like he always did when we laid together. "Get some rest then, love."

I pretended to sleep for as long as it took for Hayden to drop off and then I opened my eyes again. I took in the planes of his face, softened in sleep. I'd never get tired of watching him. Awake or asleep, he was so beautiful that it took my breath away.

He'd been about to confess his love for me, and I'd stopped him. He'd say it eventually, and I'd be forced to come to terms with my feelings.

Right there beneath the surface under the superficial layer of protection I'd put up, I knew without a single doubt that I loved him, too.

CHAPTER EIGHTEEN

The next morning, I sat in a wheelchair by the door as I waited for Hayden to pull around to the front door to pick me up. The fresh air did me good. I breathed it in deeply and only slightly winced when my wound pinched.

The police had come by early to take my statement and were as patient as could be as I relayed the entire evening to them. I didn't glance at Hayden once. I knew I'd see his anguish if I did. He blamed himself for not being there sooner, I knew it without him saying so. The guilt was on his face every time he gazed at me.

When we got to my apartment, I settled myself down onto the couch and hugged one of the throw pillows.

"I missed this couch almost as much as I missed my bed," I gushed.

Hayden's dimples curved inward with his smile. Just like every time before, the sight of his dimples knocked me on my ass.

My apartment seemed just like it had when I'd left it last Tuesday morning except for the fact that it had been cleaned. Morgan. She was the only one who had a key to my place. I made a mental note to thank her. Hayden settled in next to me, and I cuddled into his side. I tried not to think about the fact that I had mere weeks left with him and most of that would be spent recovering from being shot. What luck I had.

More than anything I wanted to drag him into the bedroom and show him how much I missed his touch. So I pulled away just enough to sit up and kissed him deeply, shoving my hand up the front of his shirt to rub my hand down his chest.

"What are you up to?" he murmured.

"Take me to bed," I demanded.

He pulled back and stared at me as if I'd lost my mind.

"You just got shot, babe. I'm not going to risk hurting you."

"We'll take it easy, it'll be fine." I reached for the button on his jeans, but he grabbed my hand and laced his fingers through mine.

"Not right now. Maybe next week if you heal up enough."

I huffed with frustration. A week was a forever when you didn't have much time with someone. "I don't think I'll make it that long." I pouted.

"Just think of it as building up anticipation," he suggested with a crooked smile.

"Can we at least lie in bed for now?"

"Yeah, we can do that, definitely."

He led me to the bedroom, and we lay under the blankets holding one another. I pressed kisses to his face and lips while he returned the sentiment. There was barely a second where our mouths weren't busy, which suited me just fine. If we were kissing, we weren't talking, and talking was the last thing I wanted to do.

We stayed there until it started to get dark out and we had to come out of our cocoon to eat. Much to my surprise and appreciation, Morgan had also stocked my fridge with food, so we made a meal out of snacks and watched TV while we ate.

There was a thick tension between Hayden and me that wouldn't go away, and I knew it was because of that L word that had been left hanging between us. I was vibrating with nervous energy, afraid he'd come right out and fully say it, leaving the ball in my court. But I think he sensed my fear or at least knew I was on edge when the day wore on and he never said it. Even when we were lying in bed that night talking.

"You're really okay," he mumbled as if he couldn't believe it.

"Of course I'm okay." I laughed. "It'll take more than one measly gunshot to keep me down," I tried to joke, but it was clear he wasn't in a joking mood.

"I could have lost you."

I could hear the entire weight of the world perched on his shoulders, weighing him down.

"Stop it, Hayden. Let's just forget all of this happened and enjoy the time we have left, okay?" It was the wrong thing to say. He just seemed even more upset.

"Right, the time we have left."

He appeared dejected, as if I'd sucker punched him right in the gut. But the horrible truth of it was, he was living in a fantasy world if he wasn't thinking about the inevitable end to our little bubble. Bubbles were meant to pop, and they could be messy when they did. I didn't think this was going to end any less messy, and that wreaked havoc in my head and heart.

I drifted off sometime around nine and didn't wake up again until late morning. Hayden had left me a note on the pillow next to me letting me know he was running out for breakfast and would be back ASAP. I took that time to call Morgan to thank her for all she'd done.

"Hello," she whispered into the receiver. "I'm in the bathroom at work, but I wasn't about to ignore your call. Is everything okay?"

"Yeah, I'm just fine." I was getting tired of everyone asking me if everything was all right, truth be told. "I just wanted to thank you for cleaning my apartment and stocking it with food. I owe you big time."

"What are you talking about?"

A silence followed as I tried to piece things together.

"When I got home yesterday my apartment was clean and I had food. You're the only one who has a key, so you can stop playing coy."

"*Oh, that.* That wasn't me. That was all Hayden. He asked for my key to your place when you were in the ICU and couldn't have visitors, so he could make things nice for you when you came home. I supplied the key, but the rest was all him. I'm telling you, the guy is in L-O-V-E with you."

I could hardly catch my breath. He had to stop doing nice things for me. It only made it harder to resist what my heart naturally wanted. "Oh, okay. I'll thank him when he gets back then." Even I could hear how flat my voice was.

"What's going on with you? You should be over the moon that he cares as much as he does. Or do you not feel the same way?"

"No, I . . . loving him would be a mistake. He's leaving, in case you've forgotten."

"Yeah, but you carried on a long-distance relationship with Drake for over a year. How is this any different?"

It was different in every way this time. I knew what it was like to be with Hayden, and if I admitted that I loved him, if I took that leap, being without him was going to feel like a special kind of hell.

"It's complicated," I answered.

"It's only complicated because you're making it complicated," she pointed out.

I scowled. A creak let me know the front door had opened then.

"I have to go, he's back."

I left the bed and pulled my robe on to go out into the

small kitchen. He stood there riffling through the bags and laying everything out on the counter. He'd stopped by the bistro where I often went with Morgan for brunch. Where he'd first asked me out. I tried not to let it choke me up.

"Morning, babe." He smiled as he kissed my forehead.

I closed my eyes and let myself feel hope for a fraction of a second, but only for a second. I knew hope was foolish in the face of all we had against us. I tried to picture waking up to forehead kisses and breakfast every day and I envied myself for having this now, knowing I wouldn't have it later.

"Good morning," I responded, trying out a smile of my own.

"I got a little bit of everything, went a little crazy."

I examined the assortment of breakfast plates and sandwiches and laughed.

"Are you feeding the army?" I joked.

He rolled his pretty black eyes to the ceiling. "You lost weight while you were in the hospital, so I'm trying to fix that."

I wasn't complaining. I had wanted to shed a few pounds for a while anyway.

"Well, thank you, it's very thoughtful of you."

One dimple imprinted his cheek as he lifted the corner of his mouth.

"Speaking of thoughtful," I said. "Thank you for cleaning and putting food in my house. You didn't have to do that."

"What else was I supposed to do while I thought you were dying?" he asked without facing me, suddenly very fixated on the food laid out on the counter.

"Hayden, don't go there, okay? We need to move past this, and that starts today. It's a new day, and I'm no longer trapped in the hospital." I took his hand and pressed a kiss to his knuckles.

He closed his eyes and breathed in deeply. "You're right,

I'm sorry." He turned his gaze to me and leaned down to kiss me.

I returned the kiss with passion, trying to prove to him that things could go back to normal as long as he'd stop dwelling on what had happened. And as long as he didn't try to tell me how he really felt about me again.

I ended up eating two egg white and cheese sandwiches, I was starving so much. After a day's diet of hospital food and six previous days of not eating, eating real food was glorious.

I was lying on the couch, my feet in Hayden's lap, and he massaged my feet as we watched TV. He still wouldn't sleep with me, not for my lack of trying. I'd tried all morning.

"It's too soon," he'd said. "You aren't healed enough."

It was a load of crap. I felt perfectly fine. I was taking my antibiotics, and they'd given me some pretty nice painkillers for the first week home. I was currently dizzy with euphoria, riding high on a wave of low dose narcotics when he suddenly dropped my foot into his lap and turned to me.

"Can we talk?"

My stomach bottomed out. This was exactly what I'd been hoping to avoid.

"Why talk when there's other things, better things, we could be doing?" I teased, hoping to distract him, but his face stayed solemn. I sighed and said, "I don't want to talk."

"It's important. I know you want to move on, but I almost lost you, Juliet. I'm still processing it, and I don't know how you can be so unmoved by it. The entire time I sat there next to your hospital bed I thought of all the things I should have said to you, all the things I should have been saying to you all along. It tortured me for six very long days. It felt like a lifetime."

Haunting pain filled his face as he recalled this past week. I couldn't pretend to know what it was like for him specifically, but I'd lost someone I'd loved once. I knew I never wanted to feel that way again. Which was why I couldn't let him say the words that were dangling off his tongue.

"You process it how you need to, and I'll process it how I need to. My method of getting over it is different than yours, clearly, but that doesn't make it wrong," I said. "I don't want to talk about it because when I do, all I can see is Carter standing over me waiting for me to die. I can still see that gun pointing right at me, knowing I had nowhere to hide, nowhere to run. Forgive me if I don't want to relive it."

I got off the couch and turned my back to him to compose myself before facing him again.

"And for the record, I lost someone once upon a time, so I understand fear and loss. I get it. I know it wasn't easy for you being so unsure about whether I'd make it or not, but that part is over. We can either agonize over it or we can spend the next few weeks making better memories to cover up the bad ones. I'll leave that choice up to you. I already made my choice." I took off to the bedroom and shut the door before he had the chance to say anything else. Obviously, I was running away. I knew he was going to keep talking, and words I wasn't prepared to hear were going to come tumbling out at my feet, and I knew I didn't have the strength to pick them up like I desperately wanted to. If our situation was different, I would have gladly listened to him tell me how he felt about me.

But our situation wasn't different. I lived here, and he lived there. Worlds away. And I wasn't about to go down that path again, not when my entire heart and sanity were at stake.

He came storming through the bedroom door, determination on his face. I sat on the edge of the bed and stared up at him. He shoved his hands through his midnight hair and paced back and forth.

"You are the most stubborn woman I've ever met, and I've met a lot of stubborn women. You give them all a run for their money, that's the goddamn truth," he ranted. "But I'm not letting you walk away from me like that. You have a problem, you bring it to me, and we work through it. Together."

"I don't have a problem," I informed him as I crossed my arms over my chest.

"Then what the fuck is going on?"

"What do you mean?"

He gave me a pointed look and said, "You've been weird ever since the hospital—no, before that. You've been pushing me away, and I want to know why."

I stood and pointed my finger into his chest. "You want to know? Fine. You're leaving in a few weeks, and I don't know if I'll ever see you again. It's all fine and dandy while we're living inside this little bubble of happiness, but that won't last forever. You'll go back to London, and I'm going to have to grieve all over again because I lost someone, only this time it's going to be so much worse. It's going to hurt like hell, and I don't know how to do it again." My voice broke on a sob, but I kept going. "I don't want you to tell me how you feel about me. If you don't say it then I can pretend I feel nothing, and hopefully that'll make it easier on me when you're gone. I don't want emotions in this. There weren't supposed to be any in the first place, Hayden. None of this was supposed to happen, but I fooled myself into thinking I could move on and still let go when I needed to. So I started letting go early. I have to protect myself. Are you happy to know the truth now? Does it change anything at all?"

An endless flow of tears poured from my eyes as I stepped away from him and pressed my fist against my mouth to stop the godawful noises coming from me. I had been so stupid to think I could put my feelings aside. No amount of pretending was going to take the pain away when he left. I was already starting to feel it, knowing what little time we had left.

"Juliet—"

"No, don't say anything," I wept, wrapping my arms around myself. When he stepped closer to me, I backed away. "Please don't touch me. I don't think I'll be able to handle it if you do."

He held his hands up to show me he was backing off, but he didn't stop there. "I won't touch you, but you're going to hear me out."

I just looked at him through blurry vision, his form distorted through the haze of tears. Maybe not being able to see him clearly would make it easier to hear what he was going to say.

"Juliet—fuck."

He paced again, from one side of the room to the other before he stopped and fixed me with a very ardent face. He sighed and threw his hands in the air.

"I love you, and I think you know that."

I sniffled and started shaking my head, but he continued.

"I fucking love you. I have for a while, and I should have told you when I first realized it. You know when I fell in love with you? It was that night neither of us slept when that prick had attacked you. You looked at me like I'd hung the fucking moon. All night you couldn't take your eyes off me, staring into mine, and I felt something move in me so strong that it scared the shit out of me. I'd never felt like that in my life. Never. I knew from the moment I laid eyes on you that I wanted you more than I'd ever wanted anything, but I didn't know that I'd end up loving you as much as I do. I'd do anything in the world for you, love."

"Then take it back," I sputtered.

"I'll do anything but that. And I think—no, I know—that under this barrier you've been putting up between us, you love me, too. You aren't really very good at hiding how you feel. Every emotion, every feeling you have, it's always there in those beautiful eyes of yours. I see the way you watch me, because I'm always watching you, too. I couldn't stop if I tried."

I wanted him to stop. It was too much, my heart breaking right down the middle with every word he spoke.

"S-stop," I pleaded, but he just kept going.

"When you look at me, it makes me want to be better than I am. I'm a stupid fuck and I do a lot of dumb shit, but you make me feel like there's so much more to me than that. I don't deserve you and I know it, but for some reason you let me in, and I don't think that was an accident or a mistake."

I dropped to the floor, the weight of all he'd said making me crumble. I ignored the shooting pain in my side. It seemed so trivial in the moment compared to what he was saying to me. Hayden was on his knees in front of me immediately.

"Tell me I'm lying. Tell me to fuck off. Just tell me something." His voice was soft as his face came into my line of sight.

I locked eyes with him, and the pure emotion in his made me burst into tears all over again.

"Why are you doing this to me" I coughed out between my hiccupping breaths.

"Baby," he whispered, taking my face in his hands, swiping at the tears on my cheeks.

My resolve was being chipped away, first by his words, then by the way he was gazing at me. I threw myself into his arms and buried my face in his neck. He lifted me off the floor and carried me to the bed. Lowering me on top of the comforter, he hung above me, observing me as if I were the most precious thing in the world before dropping beside me and rolling onto his side. I rolled halfway to meet him. When my cries died out into pathetic sniffles, I closed my eyes and tried to steady myself.

"Hayden," I began, "I'm scared."

"So am I," he admitted. "Doesn't change how I feel about you, though."

"You mean it?"

"More than I've ever meant anything." He touched me everywhere, like he couldn't bear to go without it.

"I love you, too," I whispered, and the smile he gave me was the most brilliant, earth-shattering smile I'd ever seen.

His eyes crinkled at the corners, his dimples deepened, and his lips stretched over his perfect teeth so tightly it had to have been painful. "I love you more than anything in this world," he whispered, drawing me closer to him.

His mouth found mine, and he kissed me with all the feeling he'd been holding back for so long. I was floating, that dark cloud that had been following me around finally turning into a cloud of fortune. I'd been scared of loving again after Drake, but I was hopeless when it came to Hayden.

I think I'd mostly been scared of the fall, afraid I'd flail around only to smack into the ground, never to recover. But Hayden had been right there at the bottom all along, willing and waiting to catch me. So I took the leap, right into his arms, and realized the fall wasn't so bad after all.

Chapter Nineteen

It was a week after Hayden had confessed his love to me, and I was still riding high. He'd been taking care of me, dressing my rapidly healing wound, but he also took care of my heart. He hadn't let a day pass without telling me he loved me at least a hundred times. I'd catch him looking at me, and he'd get that dimpled smile before saying, "Love you so much, babe."

It was two weeks before he'd be leaving, and the weather was finally warming, the sun baking the ground, trying to coax the flowers and plants into reviving themselves for the year. I was on my way over to Berkley's house, where Hayden was staying, for the first time ever. Typically, Hayden just stayed with me, but Berkley was going out of town for the night to play at a venue in the next town over, so we would have privacy that we'd only been able to get in my apartment.

I'd talked to the police days ago, and they'd assured me Carter wouldn't be getting out of jail anytime soon after violating a restraining order and an attempted murder charge. He'd been denied bond and he'd rot in jail until his court date. Which I'd heard was a long way off. I felt lucky to be alive, like I had a new lease on life. I was loved, I had great friends, and the sun seemed to shine a little brighter down on me. Everything I needed had been given to me.

I never did forget Drake, he was always there in the back of my mind, but that empty space I had felt in my heart next to Drake had been filled. I felt . . . happy. For the first time in a long time, I was happy.

My car bounced down a gravel driveway until a white painted farmhouse with red shutters came into view. It definitely wasn't what I had expected of Berkley, but that just had me smiling all the more. Alerted to my arrival by the obnoxious crunch of gravel, Hayden stepped out onto the porch in nothing more than a pair of low-hanging jeans. My stomach immediately flipped in desire. He still hadn't made a move to make love to me, but tonight was the night, I just knew it.

"Hey, baby," he said as I bounded up the porch steps to plant a sweet kiss on his lips. "Come on in."

When we entered, I definitely saw Berkley everywhere. The furniture was a hideous green and blue plaid that was obviously worn from years of use. Signed records adorned the walls in golden frames, and a drum set was crammed into the corner next to the TV.

"Let's go upstairs," Hayden suggested, and I followed without protest.

He pushed open his bedroom door and stood aside to let me in. The bed was large, with a navy quilt thrown over the top, and fluffy pillows lined the headboard. More band memorabilia decorated the walls, Berkley's doing I was sure. Hayden's things were scattered around the room, his boots at the bottom of the bed. I turned to him with a smile, glad he was sharing his space with me.

"I'll go grab some food for us and I'll be back."

I listened to him descend the stairs, and I stepped to the side to take in more of the room. Not looking where I was going, I backed right into the chair at the small desk and knocked a messenger bag over. The contents spilled out, and I cursed before dropping down to begin picking everything up to shove back into the bag, but then I froze.

There among the random papers and manila folders were

opened letters. Letters that carried my handwriting. My letters to Drake.

I was confused more than anything, but something ugly twisted deep in my gut. There had to be some rational explanation for why Hayden had those letters, but nothing came to mind. Hayden clonked back upstairs, and I spun on my heel with the pile of letters in my hands. When he saw me holding them, he stopped in the doorway.

"Why . . . how do you have these?" I squeaked out.

"Let me explain."

"You'd better. There's no way you should have these. What the hell is going on?"

He looked panicked and lost as he set the plates of food on the dresser and put a hand to his mouth, like he was about to throw up. He dragged his hand down past his chin until it slid from his face altogether.

"Hayden," I said, sounding hysterical. "Explain. Now."

He nodded as if resigning himself to what was about to happen. "Drake, I knew him."

"You *knew* him?"

"He was my little brother. When he died we hadn't spoken in nearly three years, but he still left everything to me for some reason. I guess he didn't really have anyone else to leave it to. When I was going through his things to figure out what needed to go, I came across these letters from some girl he'd been talking to, and then I came across her pictures on his computer. And I knew then that I needed to meet her. After the words she'd written down on paper and mailed to my little brother, I couldn't not know her."

I stood there paralyzed. I could hardly believe what he was saying, but he wasn't done.

"So once everything was settled with his properties and accounts, I hopped on a plane to North Carolina. It happened that I had friends there. I didn't tell them what I was up to. I knew they'd try to talk me out of it, but I had to do it.

"I'd seen you a handful of times before I finally gathered up the courage to approach you in a dingy bar, and with the first words you spoke to me, I was a goner. I liked you already. I had every intention of telling you who I was, but I fucked that up royally because I didn't know how to just be honest about who I was. I guess a part of me was afraid that if I told you, then you'd run, and that was the last thing I wanted. So I tried to be your friend, but it evolved into something more so fast that I missed every window of opportunity to come clean until it seemed like it was too late. I felt so guilty, but before I knew it, I was in love with you and I couldn't let go like I knew I should have. I should have just let you get on with your life. I didn't belong in it, I never did. But I'm a selfish bastard and I wanted whatever you'd give me. Every day that passed I looked at you and knew that you'd figure it out one day, but I still couldn't bring myself to divulge the truth. I thought . . . I don't know what I thought. I lied by omission, and for that, I'm so goddamn sorry. I'll never forgive myself for keeping it from you, and all I can do at this point is hope for the best, I guess."

My lip was trembling in heartbreak and anger. I let the letters slip through my shaking hands until they hit the floor with a steady string of *thwacks*. My gaze was locked on his, and I hoped my eyes conveyed every ounce of fury and hurt I felt.

"You . . . I . . . you lied to me," I said weakly, my lungs deflated in betrayal.

"Juliet—"

"You fucking *lied to me!*" I picked up the nearest object to my left, a paperweight, and chucked it at him, barely missing my target, his head. "You son of a bitch!"

"Juliet, please—"

"Don't you dare say my name like you know me. All of this" —I gestured between us—"is over." I laughed humorlessly and ran a hand through my hair, bewildered. "I'm such a fucking idiot. To think someone would just fall into my lap and understand what I was going through without batting an eye."

I picked up a *Battle of the Bands* trophy and threw it as hard as I could. It pelted him in the chest, but he didn't even flinch.

"You're a sorry bastard for making me fall in love with you when everything, *everything* I thought I had with you was built on one big lie. How *dare* you? How fucking dare you do that to me? How could you?" My anger was starting to give way to my heartbreak, and I cried, my eyes screwing up with burning tears. "How could you do that to me? How could you crawl into my bed knowing that you were lying to me about something this massive? Was it all just some game to you? Take a broken woman and break her down even more?"

"Nothing about you was a joke to me, love."

"Don't call me that," I snapped, jerking a pillow off the bed and throwing it at him. I knew it wouldn't hurt him, but it still made me feel better. "Don't you ever call me that again. I hate you! I hate you so much."

He said nothing while I stood there throwing all the pillows on his bed at him. I was having the worst meltdown of my life right in front of the man who had ripped my heart out and stomped all over it, and I had never been more humiliated.

When there was nothing left to throw, I tried to push past him, but he grabbed my arms.

"Don't fucking touch me. You disgust me."

He released me, though I could see it killed him to do it. I shoved past him and ran down the stairs and out the front door to my car. I turned my car around and caught sight of him in the rearview mirror, standing there looking like he'd lost everything worth living for. Good. I wanted him to know what true pain felt like. He deserved far worse.

On my way home I dialed Morgan's number, but I was so incoherent that she said she'd meet me at my apartment and hung up. I sped home, ignoring the speed limit signs, and screeched into a parking spot in front of my building. I ran up the stairs, taking them two at a time and let myself into my apartment. I was barely in the door when Morgan came bounding in.

I was curled up on the floor sobbing, and she dropped down to gather me up in her arms. She hugged me tightly and let me get it all out before she asked me anything at all. When I had calmed down some, she moved me to the couch while she went to fetch the hard liquor. She returned with a glass that I downed in no time, and I reached for the bottle to drink from it, ignoring the glass altogether.

"What the hell happened?" she asked, worry lining every feature.

"Hayden. He's a lying, scumbag, piece-of-shit asshole."

"Okay," she drew out. "Start from the top."

I told her everything about my discovering the letters and his long explanation for why he'd duped me. By the time I finished, I felt empty. I'd gone through fury and heartache, and now I felt nothing at all. I was numb, and I wasn't so sure it was all thanks to the whiskey.

"What the fuck," Morgan whispered into the air. "Did Berkley know about this?"

"No, he said he didn't tell his friends here what he was up to. So Berkley is off the hook for now."

Morgan just sat there with her mouth opening and closing in shock. "I don't even know what to say, Juliet. I can't believe it. They don't even look alike. And they don't have the same last name either. How is this possible?"

"I don't know, I didn't take the time to ask for the details of their family life between calling him names and throwing everything I could get my hands on at him," I replied sarcastically. Thinking back, I recalled the first night I'd met Hayden. He'd told me he had a little brother and that they'd had different fathers. I assumed that was the explanation for it, but it hardly mattered at this point.

"Sweetie, I am *so* sorry. I'll go kill him right now if you want. I'll string him up in the parking lot and flay him alive."

"And take away my chance to do it? No way." I laughed maniacally, taking another swallow from the bottle. "How could I have been so stupid, Morgan?"

"You weren't stupid. You were trying to move on with your life, and there's nothing wrong with that. What he did is reprehensible, and I would be your alibi if you wanted to set his house on fire, but you aren't the stupid one in this scenario. Don't even think about blaming yourself." She grabbed my hands and squeezed them in hers.

"I let him into my life, into my bed. All the while he was hiding this massive secret from me that he's really my dead boyfriend's brother. How could he look at me and tell me he loved me all those times when he was lying about who he was?" I couldn't fathom the whys or hows of how his mind worked. For all I knew he was a sociopath and my whole relationship with him had been some elaborate prank.

My phone rang, and I didn't even have to check it to know who it was. I silenced it, but moments later it chimed with a text. Through eyes glazed over by alcohol and anguish, I read the message and wished I hadn't.

Juliet, please. I can't take back what I've done, but I love you more than life, and I meant it every time I've said it. Can you just talk to me?

It was like my heart was breaking all over again as I typed out a drunken message and hit Send.

Fuck off, asshole.

I didn't wait long for his reply.

Call me whatever you want, but give me a chance to fix this.

There is no fixing this. You crushed me then ground me into the dirt like I was nothing.

You deserve a lot better than what I've done, and I'm going to spend every second of my life trying to make up for it.

Morgan snatched my phone away from me and started typing away. When she appeared satisfied, she sent the message and handed my phone back to me. I glanced down and read what she'd written and teared up.

This is Morgan. Juliet doesn't want to talk to you. You've done enough damage, now leave her alone so I can help her pick up the pieces in peace. You owe her that much at least.

Hayden didn't message back, and I assumed it was because Morgan's message had been loud and clear. I felt drained and beyond drunk. I needed my bed.

"I'm going to sleep. I need to forget about today for at least ten hours."

She nodded and informed me that she was sleeping on the couch. She wanted to be close but still give me alone time to process everything I'd discovered.

I lay there in the dark, clutching my aching chest, and cried into my pillow. My pillow that still smelled of mint and soap. His scent seemed to cling to everything I owned, and I could still feel him everywhere. It was so easy to recall the way his hands felt on my body, how his mouth felt against mine. I should have pushed the memories aside, but I let them in and I let them swallow me up.

I thought back to the night of our first date at Berkley's concert where he'd tried to kiss me. I'd wanted him even then, but I'd fought it so hard. I had still been in love with Drake and it seemed wrong then. The memory of the first time I'd made love to Hayden fluttered by. It had been exquisite, like coming home after a long, exhausting trip. Now it just felt tainted.

Then I recalled the evening of Carter's attack, when Hayden said he'd fallen in love with me. I'd worked so hard then to etch his face into my brain that I couldn't get it out now. I could so easily picture the perfect planes of his face set with contentment, the way his black eyes stared right into the very depths of me, and those damned dimples that appeared when he smiled. Thinking back, I saw that love in his eyes as he'd gazed me all night long while he'd caressed me. But it couldn't have been real love. Real love didn't hurt like this.

And finally, I remembered telling him I loved him. How I wished I could take it back now. He didn't deserve to hear those words from me.

I stared out the window up at the moon while I huddled in the middle of the bed, hugging myself for comfort. How was I going to move past this? It had taken months for the pain of losing Drake to lessen, but this was a whole different story, a whole different dragon to slay. What I'd had with Hayden had been tangible and electric. I realized somewhere along the way that I'd loved Drake because he'd been a safe bet. He'd been an excellent man, but there was no on-the-edge-of-my-seat excitement like there'd been with Hayden. Drake would have taken care of me, I knew that, but he wouldn't have given me passion and exhilaration. They might have been brothers, but they couldn't have been more different.

When the whiskey started wearing off and the headache set in, I let myself lie there in pain. Physical pain meant I was feeling something other than emotional turmoil and mental agony. I'd take what I could get at this point.

Light streamed in through the window when the sun rose, and I pulled myself out of bed. It was Wednesday, and I needed to go to work. They'd given me the rest of the week to heal after I'd been gunned down in front of the building by a former employee, but I was ready to go back. I needed to find normal again, get back in the swing of things. If I stayed home until Monday, I'd just wallow in self-pity, and that wasn't healthy for anyone.

I took a long, hot shower, scrubbing Hayden off myself completely for good before getting dressed and applying my makeup. I didn't really feel like dressing up, but this was what I'd done before Hayden, so it was what I'd do after him.

When I stepped into the kitchen, Morgan was already up making coffee.

She turned to me and did a double take. "What are you doing?"

"Going to work," I replied with more enthusiasm than I felt.

"Are you sure that's a good idea? You've been through hell lately, and no one would blame you for taking some time to deal with it."

"I'm sure. I need to move on, and that starts with going back to work like I do every Monday through Friday." I poured myself a cup of coffee and dumped cream and sugar into it, stirring before I took a sip. It burned my tongue, but again, physical pain was currently welcome.

"Okay, I need to run home to change, but I'll come back over, and we can ride together."

"Don't worry about it, I'll be fine to drive. I'll just see you at lunch." I didn't want to lean on someone else to get me through this. If being best friends with Morgan had taught me anything, it was that I was stronger than I let myself believe. I just had to tap into my strength, shove it all down, and power on.

She stared at me a moment as if assessing me. "I'll see you at lunch, then." She hugged me in passing and then I was alone.

I finished my coffee, grabbed my purse, and headed out the door to greet the brand-new day head-on.

Chapter Twenty

I got to the bottom of the steps and nearly walked right into someone.

"Sorry about that. I wasn't paying attention. I'm clums—" I stopped when I realized I'd almost walked right into Hayden.

"Juliet," he tried to say, but I interrupted him.

"What are you doing here?" I ground out, taking a step back. My head was throbbing, and my chest was tight with loneliness. Being around him was a bad idea.

I took a moment to appraise him, and he seemed no better than I did. Even with makeup on I was frightful to see. He had the same tired expression on his face that I did.

"You need to leave," I stated with a cold blankness to my voice.

"Please, talk to me," he begged, as if he were close to getting on his knees in front of me to plead forgiveness.

While the thought appealed to me, it wouldn't change my mind.

"I don't have anything to say to you. I'm going to be late for work, so if you don't mind, I'm going to go now." I stepped past him and unlocked my car.

"I thought you were off until Monday."

"Well, the rest of my week off was ruined by this asshole who took advantage of me, so I decided to return early."

At least he had the decency to appear ashamed. I got into my car and drove off, leaving him standing there all alone.

I tried not to look at him as I stepped hard on the pedal,

but I glanced into the mirror and saw him hanging his head. Something akin to pity tugged at my heart, and I mentally kicked myself. I shouldn't feel sorry for him. He was the one who did *me* dirty, not the other way around. Either way, I couldn't deny that he still affected me. Seeing him again, especially so soon after discovering who he really was, had been like a slap to the face. It pulled me out of my stupor and stirred up feelings I'd been setting off to the side. Try and deny it all I wanted, I still loved him. I didn't hate him at all like I'd told him I did. And that revelation pissed me off.

When I got to work, I slammed my door angrily, the sound echoing in the underground garage. My heels clacked against the concrete when I stomped to the elevator. Once I reached my floor, I swept into the office. I was glad to see that there weren't many people there yet, but the ones who were just stared at me. Everyone knew by now that I was the one involved in the Carter scandal. How else would they explain me being shot the same night Carter had been arrested for shooting the woman he'd previously assaulted?

"Juliet? My office."

I turned. Ms. Fisher entered her office. I went in behind her and shut the door.

She stood before her desk, leaning against it casually. "What are you doing here?"

"I'm ready to come back to work. Get back on track." I tried to smile, but it felt strained and false.

She appraised me carefully while she thought it over. "Your leave was mandatory, you know," she pointed out. "Have you seen the therapist we suggested?"

"No, not yet. They couldn't squeeze me in until tomorrow." In reality, I'd forgotten to make the appointment until a few days ago.

"Well, do see to it that you go. If he thinks you're fit to return to work then we'll talk, but for now I need you to go home. In truth, you being here after such a recent traumatic event is a bit of a liability. I'm sure you understand."

My heart sank. I was counting on today being the day I began to get my life together.

"Of course," I said anyway. My shoulders slumped, and I left her office, ignoring the stares of my coworkers. I got onto the elevator and rode it back down to the garage. I sat in my car, frustration bubbling up inside me. I just wanted my life back. Pre-Hayden and pre-Drake, back when I was content with my life and nothing bad had happened.

I drove aimlessly for a while before I found myself at the park. It was still early, so no one was out other than early joggers and a handful of elderly folks carrying binoculars while they fed the birds. Taking a familiar path I'd once been down with Hayden, I stopped in the little alcove where we'd picnicked together, the first time he'd truly touched me intimately. I could still feel his hand between my legs when he'd hiked up my dress and stuck his hand down my pants.

Clenching my fists against the searing hurt, I went back to the path and took the loop a few times. I walked fast, wired by the coarse edge that had settled in my bones. But when more people entered the park, I left. I didn't want to be around a lot of people right now. Especially not happy people. Happy people currently made me sick.

I slouched down in my seat in the car and pressed my forehead to the steering wheel. There was nowhere I could go where I could be around other people who knew better than to be so excited for life in front of me. Everywhere I went I'd have to see perfect couples with their perfect children in their perfect families. It was a glaring reminder that I'd probably end up alone for the rest of my life. There was no way I could put my trust in another man after what Hayden had done.

Turning the key over in the ignition, I pulled away and drove. I drove so much I ended up in Haversdale, a city four hours away. Somewhere no one knew me. I kind of liked the idea of no one knowing me.

This city was much bigger than the one I lived in, a little intimidating, but soon enough I found my way around. I parked in a garage and ambled down a busy sprawling street. For hours I checked out all the cool shops and boutiques, buying Morgan a really pretty dangly bracelet from a shop where they were handcrafted. It had a little dragonfly hanging from it, her favorite insect. I never did ask why she had a favorite insect. I thought maybe it was just one of her strange quirks.

At four in the afternoon I decided it was close enough to evening to find a bar with a stool that had my name written all over it. I turned down the next street and found a small bar called The Mint Frog. I chose it mostly because I liked the name, even if it reminded me of the way Hayden smelled.

As I walked in, a few curious gazes drifted over me before everyone got back to their drinks and conversation. I sat on a stool at the bar and waited for the bartender to come over. He was well-built and purposely bald, a gold hoop in his left ear. When he approached he smiled, and when maybe two years ago I would have flirted with him some, now I just saw the potential to get screwed over again.

"Whiskey on the rocks, please." I didn't need a mixer tonight. Whiskey straight up it was.

Seeming to notice my distress, he said, "What's bothering you, darlin'?"

I gave him a world-weary expression. "The entirety of maledom sucks."

"Ah, man troubles. I apologize on behalf of men everywhere for whatever fool was stupid enough to hurt you."

He was definitely flirting, but I didn't care. I didn't want him, and even if I was thinking of a rebound, it wouldn't happen in a bar. That was how Hayden had fooled me, and I decided I was going to be smarter than that next time around. If there even was a next time.

"Thanks," I said, pushing my glass toward him for a refill after swallowing the entire contents.

"A girl after my own heart." He laughed and filled it up more this time.

He moved down the bar as new patrons took stools, but I caught him watching me with open concern. There was no reason he should worry. He didn't even know me. No one here knew me. All the more reason to get plastered and forget Hayden and the total devastation he'd caused for a while.

Two hours later I was clutching the bar to steady myself. I felt like I was going to slip off my stool at any moment. The bartender was standing in front of me, cracking a smile at my obvious drunkenness.

"You're cut off for the rest of the night, sweetie," he announced.

I groaned. "Just one more," I begged. If I blacked out, so be it. It would be hours without pain, and that was what I needed more than anything. I hadn't slept in over thirty hours, but I didn't think sleep would come to me easily again.

"Wish I could, but you're barely clinging on as it is. Give me a number, and I'll call someone to come pick you up."

Morgan was going to kill me. She wouldn't even get here until ten at night, which put us home sometime after two. I still gave him Morgan's number, and he pulled a phone out from under the bar, punched in the number, then held the phone to his ear. "Yes, this is Porter from The Mint Frog in Haversdale. I have a friend of yours here, and she needs a ride home." He paused and glanced at me. "Your name Juliet?"

I nodded and regretted it immediately. It felt like my whiskey-soaked brain was swimming around in my skull.

"Yep, Juliet. Okay, I'll let her know."

"Is she coming" I asked after he'd hung up.

"Yes, but she also said she was going to kick your ass."

I figured as much. I simply shrugged and continued to hold on to the bar to steady myself.

"She must be a good friend to drive four hours to pick you up."

"She's the best," I slurred with a confident smile. I would be next to nothing without the fierce loyalty of our friendship over all these years. "So, Porter, is it?"

"Yeah, that's what people call me anyway." He slid a glass of ice-cold water in front of me. "You need to sober up some," he explained.

"I'd rather not," I admitted and groaned, dropping my head to the bar.

"Want to talk about it?"

I was going to say no, but something stopped me. If anyone could give me some insight into the mind of a guy it was, well, another guy. So I started from the beginning, with Drake, and when I finished with finding out that Hayden was Drake's brother all along, Porter let out a low whistle.

"That's some soap opera shit right there."

"Tell me about it. My life hasn't been normal since that devil walked into it." It had been a wild ride, not all of it good, but not all of it bad either. Though the bad outweighed the good to a large degree right now. "What would you do if you were in my position?"

"Honestly? I'd listen to what he had to say for closure's sake, then I'd try to move on with my life. Fool me once, shame on you. Fool me twice, shame on me. I couldn't give someone another chance to mess with my head like that."

I nodded, coming to the same conclusion, though it hadn't occurred to me to listen to what Hayden had to say. I had just wanted him to disappear. But it was true that I wasn't feeling closure and I desperately needed it. That morning in front of my apartment wasn't the last time I'd see him, I was sure, so next time he came around I'd hear him out and get everything off my chest as well, then I'd cut him from my life for good. A clean break with no regrets hanging over my head.

I was still buzzing from the alcohol in my veins when I heard my name. I turned. Morgan strode in followed by Berkley . . . and Hayden. My breath caught in my throat, and I quickly looked away.

"One of them him?" Porter asked, leaning across the bar.

"The tall one with the dark hair," I confirmed.

Porter sized him up and nodded but didn't say anything more.

"Come on, you crazy bitch, let's get you home." Morgan sighed, placing her hand around my upper arm.

"Why is he here?" I asked with an accusing tone. Why would she bring him along?

"I was hanging out with Berkley at his house, then Hayden came home when bartender dude called and said you were piss drunk in a bar four hours from town, and he refused to get out of the car."

I dragged myself off the barstool only to pitch forward and nearly fall flat on my face. It seemed my soberness had been an illusion built upon by sitting perfectly still for hours, because I got my second wind of boozy headrush immediately upon standing.

Berkley and Morgan each wrapped one of my arms around their shoulders and began walking me out.

"Come back again soon, sweetness," Porter called out.

I flashed him a smile. When my gaze drifted to Hayden, he was glaring holes into the bartender. I might have reveled in knowing he was jealous of what he'd never have again.

"Where's your car?" Morgan asked when we stepped out into the fresh March air.

"Um, it's in a parking garage somewhere." I pulled the little ticket from my back pocket and squinted down at it with one eye closed, trying to read it. "Borough Avenue Parking Garage. That's . . ." I looked left and right and pointed in either direction. "I'm not sure where that is."

"For fuck's sake," Morgan grumbled. "Come on, we'll find it."

"I love you so much, Morgan, you know that, right," I gushed while she and Berkley continued hauling me down the sidewalk.

"I love you, too," she breathed, the labor of half dragging my dead weight taking its toll.

"You're the best friend ever."

"And you reek of whiskey. How much did you drink tonight?" She didn't sound angry with me, but worried.

I never drank like this, and this would make the second night in a row I'd gotten totally plastered.

"Oh, I don't know, like a whole bottle I'd say," I tried to say nonchalantly.

"Jesus Christ," Hayden muttered behind us.

"Shut up, you. I don't want you to give me any more grief than you already have," I shouted over my shoulder.

He said nothing more after that. I could almost feel his guilt, it was so palpable. I hoped it was eating him alive.

We took street after street until we finally stopped to ask for directions. We were heading in the right direction at least, three streets over from the garage. They continued dragging me along, and my stomach rolled.

"Wait," I protested, quickly detaching myself from them

and, bent at the waist, emptying my stomach in the street.

When I straightened up, they took me by my arms again and plodded on. The parking garage came into view, and after guessing what floor my car was on twice before I got it right, we finally made it. Morgan dug around in my pocket for the key and unlocked the passenger door, shoving me into the seat.

"You guys go ahead, I'll get her home," Morgan said, almost closing my door.

"You can't carry her up two flights of stairs," Hayden pointed out.

I hated that he was right.

"I'll crawl up the damn stairs if I have to." I laughed, throwing my head back against the seat. I was a happy drunk usually, last night being the exception, but that was when the pain had been fresh. I'd had a little time to process things, and my drunken mask of joy was firmly tucked into place now.

"I'll take her home," Hayden offered.

I was just about to protest vehemently when I got this brilliant idea that I knew I was going to regret. "Fine, we need to talk anyway," I said with a passive wave of my hand.

Morgan turned to me in disbelief. "Are you sure about this?"

"Totally. How much more damage could he possibly do at this point anyway?"

"If you're sure," she uneasily said, slipping the keys into Hayden's hand and got up in his face. "You hurt her, you do *anything* wrong, and I will personally gut you." She leaned down into the car and kissed my cheek. "Let me know when you get home. Come on, Berkley."

The pair of new friends walked away. Hayden gently shut my door and came around the car. We pulled from the spot and wove our way through the maze of the garage. I had a long, four-hour car ride ahead of me and I had a lot to say. I'd hear him out, then I'd unleash holy hell down upon him until he thought twice before ever looking at another woman with the intention to deceive them again.

I was a woman scorned, and as the saying goes, hell hath no fury like a woman scorned.

Chapter Twenty-One

The first hour of the car ride was full of quiet tension. He looked strained, like he was holding himself back. I was tired of the pretense, so I turned to him.

"Go ahead and say what you have to say, I'm listening." I still had that slight drunken warble to my voice, and I knew the scent of whiskey had to be overpowering in the small cabin of my car.

"I'll wait," he stated, turning up the radio.

I smashed my hand against the power button. Not due to being irritated, though I was, but the button was broken, and hitting it was the only way to turn it off.

"I don't want to wait. I want to get this over with so I can go home and go to bed," I snapped.

"I miss you," he mumbled, almost as if to himself.

"Wish I could say the same," I shot back.

He sighed and kept driving. It became apparent after fifteen minutes that he wasn't going to say anything more. I didn't know what he was waiting for. It didn't make a difference when it was said. All that mattered was that we cleared the air between us so we could walk away from this without any doubts that we'd gotten everything off our chests.

The next three hours were agonizingly quiet, but I was as lost in thought as Hayden. Maybe he was trying to figure out exactly what to say to me like I was trying to pin down the words I needed to say to him. Or maybe he was just avoiding the topic since we were stuck in the car together.

As we pulled into the lot in front of my building, I swung the door open and tumbled out. Hayden was rounding the car, trying to hold me up, within seconds.

"Don't touch me," I griped, ripping my arm away and stumbling back into the car. The four hours had done nothing to clear the fog from my head. "I can walk."

Mimicking a newborn deer, I strutted across the parking lot in my work heels, my knees clashing together every couple of steps. I somehow made it to the stairs, and when I looked up, I felt dizzy. There were so many of them. I didn't think I could do it, but I'd said I'd crawl if I had to, so I fell over onto the stairs and started pulling myself up.

"Jesus," Hayden cursed, lifting me up off the stairs into his arms and ascending.

"Put me down," I cried, beating my fists against him.

He ignored my demands to be released until we were standing at my door. Using my keys, he unlocked the door, and we went inside. I whirled on him, gazing up into those stormy dark eyes that I'd stared into with adoration so many times. I had to glance away when everything he felt, everything he needed to say, stared right back at me.

"Juliet—"

"Say what you need to say, Hayden. I'll give you five minutes, then you're going to listen to what I have to say."

Not wasting the precious time I'd given him, he began. "I fucked up. I fucked up the one thing that ever truly mattered to me, and nothing I could ever say to you would tell you how sorry I am. At first I was scared you wouldn't want to talk to me if you knew who I was, but later I was afraid you'd run away from me. By that point, I already loved you so much." He bit out a hollow laugh. "You ended up running anyway, so I guess it doesn't matter now. You're the best thing that ever could have happened to me, Juliet. I don't really conform to any kind of religion, but I still thanked God every day for giving you to me." He pinched his mouth in his hand and pressed on. "I never in my life thought anyone would mean so much to me. Though he'd washed his hands of me, I still loved Drake. He was my little brother, and I still checked in on him from time to time to make sure he was doing all right. Just to find out after he died that he was doing better than all right because he had you. I would apologize for reading those letters, but I'm not sorry. If I hadn't, I never would have met you, and regardless of how things played out, I can't regret that, for a while, I had you. You're brilliant and funny and beautiful, everything I'd ever wanted in a partner. So I am sorry that I've caused you so much pain, but I'm not sorry for meeting you. Meeting you was the greatest pleasure life could have offered me."

I swallowed down the emotion that had lodged itself in my throat and looked down at my feet. Beautiful words from a beautiful man, but I couldn't just let go of what he'd done.

"Please say something, love," he pleaded.

When I tilted my head up again, I squared my shoulders, and a single tear rolled down my cheek. I didn't want to cry, but along with being a relatively happy drunk, I was also an emotional one.

"What you did, Hayden . . . I've never felt so hurt in my life. I thought losing Drake had been painful, and for a while after, I thought I'd be broken forever. Then you came along and showed me that I could let go a little, move on with my life. Just to throw it back in my face. I feel so betrayed and heartbroken. I've never felt like this before, ever, and I don't know how to get over it. You're still stuck in my head on a damn loop, every single memory and smile and laugh I've ever had with you just replaying like some kind of movie I'm being forced to watch for the rest of my life. Losing

Drake hurt a lot, but losing you the way I did, *that* is what finally broke me. You'd made me believe that I could love again, and then you took my heart and shredded it to pieces right in front of me. And I want to hate you. I want to hate you so much, but the truth is that I don't. I still love you, and because of that I just end up hating myself for being an idiot. My only solace is knowing that you'll be gone soon, and you won't be hanging around haunting me forever. Maybe one day I'll get over it, but it won't be anytime soon. It's going to feel like a festering wound for a long time, and I'm trying to prepare myself for that. So I'm asking—no, I'm begging you—don't come around anymore. Let me start the process of healing from this so I can maybe one day have a normal life again. If you owe me anything at all, you owe me the chance to start over."

My voice was trembling by the time I finished, hoarse with unshed tears that I was struggling to hold back. Just when I thought I didn't have any more tears left in me, they would sneak up on me.

"I'm leaving later today. In about"—he checked his watch—"seven hours."

The news didn't bring me relief like I'd thought it would. I felt panic and fear. He was leaving. This was it. I'd never see him again, and while I should be glad, my insides just waged war instead. My heart seized up, my head felt stuffed full of cotton, my legs weak. I reached out to clutch the breakfast bar counter and fell, banging my cheek on the corner, and I let out a howl of pain.

"Shit." Hayden helped me stand and immediately moved into the kitchen to fill a bag with ice and wrapped it in a paper towel. He brought it up to my cheek, cupping the other side of my face with his other hand.

I stared up at him and felt so conflicted.

I needed to hate him for what he'd done, but I couldn't

find hate for him inside me anywhere, and I searched deep. He'd taken a piece of me and still carried it with him. I'd always have a tie to him that I'd probably never manage to sever. I'd ache forever, I was sure of it. But the cold, hard truth was that he'd lied to me, kept a huge secret from me that had rocked me. It was unforgiveable, and for that reason alone, I needed to let him go.

Hayden pulled the makeshift ice pack away and examined my cheek. "It's going to be bruised, but I think you'll make it." He smiled a little, letting me see those dimples one last time before they'd be gone from my life forever.

He didn't let go of my face, but instead lowered his head and pressed his lips against mine. It would have been so easy to fall into his arms and pretend for just tonight that nothing had happened to disrupt the steady balance I thought I'd found, but I had more respect for myself than that, even drunk. I pulled away and pursed my lips. His eyes briefly closed before zeroing in on me again.

"I'm sorry, I shouldn't have done that."

"No, you shouldn't have," I agreed, and all while my heart was screaming, *please, kiss me again!* But I had switched to brain mode, leaving my heart far behind me, and my brain was telling me to kick him out before anything more happened.

"I'll go now, if you think you'll be okay?" He seemed hesitant to leave, and I knew why. We were both painfully aware that it would be the last time we ever saw one another.

"I'll be fine."

He nodded, licked his lips, and moved to pass me. He stopped by my side, turned his head toward me, and said, "I'll always love you, Juliet. It's you, or it's nobody."

I continued to stand there long after the front door closed behind him. The ice pack melted, sending rivulets of condensation into a puddle on the counter. My face hurt badly, and, well, everything hurt if I was being honest.

It wasn't until I was lying in bed that I let myself cry again. My pillows no longer smelled like him, and that crushed me. I wanted comfort, comfort that only he'd ever brought me. How horrible it was to need comfort from the very person who had caused my distress in the first place.

I didn't sleep. I stayed up watching my clock, waiting for nine-thirty, the time of his flight. When the time came, my chest felt heavy, like something unmovable had settled in on it and refused to leave me. My eyes were puffy from crying all night, my nose still dripping into the tissues I pressed against it.

Earlier in the morning I'd sent Morgan a message to let her know I was home and that I was okay, but I wasn't okay. I didn't think I'd be okay ever again.

At ten forty-three there was a knock on my door, and I had this stupid hope that he hadn't left after all. He'd told me he wasn't going to give up, but leaving meant giving up. I peeked through the little eye hole in the door. Berkley stood there. That glimmer of hope I'd had died out, vanished as I opened the door.

"Jesus, have you slept at all, Jules?" He pushed past me into the apartment and sat on the couch, throwing his arm over the back.

"What are you doing here?"

"Checking in on you. Clearly you need someone, to because you look like you've been chewed up and spit out."

"You really know how to make a girl feel special, Berkley." The corners of my mouth twitched when he smiled at me.

"He told me everything, you know. For the record, I think what he did was fucked and I almost kicked his ass for it, but you have to know he really does love you. That part at least wasn't a lie."

"Berkley," I sighed. "It doesn't matter anymore."

"And why the hell not? You're both so stubborn that you can't set everything to the side and just *really* think about what you're giving up. I watched him after you left, the way he moped around, not eating, not sleeping. If it weren't for the fact that I've been in love myself before, I'd almost think it was pathetic. And you. Drinking yourself into a coma over it. You're both just hurting yourselves even more."

I'd never heard Berkley so passionate about anything before except for maybe his music. It was like someone had dumped a bucket of ice-cold water over me. I felt chilled to the bone.

"How am I supposed to forgive him for what he did?"

"That's what you do when you love someone," he said quietly. "You forgive their fuck-ups and work through it together. It was pretty gross watching you two, but I know that what you had together was real. Everyone could see it. From that first night at the bowling alley I watched him watch you, and I'd never seen him look at anyone like that before in all the years I've known him. I fucking knew he was a goner even then. And you're no different in the way you stare at him. So stop being a fucking moron and sort your shit out."

He stood then and grabbed me by my shoulders.

"Just think about what I said, okay? Don't waste your life trying to let go of something that was meant to happen." He cuffed me under the chin, winked, and left my apartment.

All day I turned it over in my head, everything Berkley had said, but it seemed useless at this point. Hayden was on his way back to London, maybe even already there by now. There was an entire ocean separating us, and my only option at this point was to let it all go, even if it didn't feel right.

Hayden had made his choice by leaving. It was a clear

signal that he'd given up on me, and he'd given up so easily at that. Berkley was wrong about it all. A piece of me still loved Hayden, I knew that, but I couldn't just act on it on a whim. I needed to be sure, and I wasn't sure. Not so soon after his betrayal. Maybe with time it would start to make sense to me. Or maybe it wouldn't. I didn't know.

I had my first therapy session, then Morgan came by after work with Chinese takeout. We watched TV, ranted about work, and stayed far from booze. Maybe the only thing Berkley had been right about had been my excessive drinking over the past few nights, so I was taking it easy.

With Morgan as a distraction, I could almost pretend things were normal. Almost. It didn't take long before Hayden's face appeared in my mind, filling me both with deep sadness and longing.

"Berkley said he came by today," Morgan brought up, biting into her fortune cookie.

"Yeah, just for a minute." I shrugged, trying to make light of it.

"I don't agree with his methods, but his sentiments aren't far off the mark, are they?" She peered at me curiously.

I threw my hands up in the air. "So I still love Hayden, big deal. It doesn't change what he did. He's in London now, I'm here. We can both start moving on with our lives. That's just the way it is." I cracked open my fortune cookie and shoved a piece into my mouth as I read the little slip of paper and scoffed.

Love, because it is the only true adventure.

What a joke.

Morgan picked up my fortune that I'd thrown on the coffee table and read it with a sly tilt of her lips. "See, even the fortune cookie knows!"

"What happened to flaying Hayden alive in the parking lot?" I asked defensively.

"That was before I knew you still loved him."

"Does it really make that big a difference if I do?"

"It makes all the difference," she answered cryptically.

When she left I downed a sleeping pill. I honestly needed my rest. My therapist was sending his notes over to Ms. Fisher after I'd left for review to see if I was fit to return to work. I thought it had gone well and I was expecting to be back to work by Friday. Things were going to fall into place again, I just needed to get up this hill I'd been climbing.

With a head no longer foggy from whiskey, I was able to think more clearly. I lay awake for the next thirty minutes going over every agonizing detail of the past few days as the sleeping pills finally took effect.

Chapter Twenty-Two

One month later

I was meeting Morgan for lunch by the food truck. She'd messaged me that morning telling me she had something exciting to tell me, and I hoped to God it wasn't that she'd gotten back together with Mark. Then again, maybe I was a bit cynical.

Thirty-two days had passed since I'd last seen Hayden, but the pain hadn't lessened any. If anything, it just felt like the hole in my chest had grown, gaping open. I wasn't angry anymore, which had to be an improvement, but I missed him a lot. And damn me, but I still loved him as much as I had a month ago. I busied myself constantly so I didn't have time to stop and think about it. I'd become pretty reliant on the sleeping pills, but it seemed like a small price to pay if it brought me solace.

Morgan had been pushing me to date again, but I was nowhere near ready. It had taken me over three months to recover from Drake, who I now thought of with warm nostalgia, but Hayden was going to take a lot longer. My heart still belonged to him in every way.

I found myself often wondering what he was doing, but I'd stop myself before it veered into *who is he doing* territory. Those thoughts brought me nothing but misery.

"Hey, lovely, having a good day?"

I looked up as Morgan approached. "It's a day," I responded before elaborating. "Ms. Fisher is seriously the worst. I have to finish so many files that I'll probably be here all night."

Morgan frowned and fidgeted. "Well, actually, I was hoping you'd come see Berkley's band with me tonight. He said they have new songs to play, and I'm pretty pumped about it."

If I wasn't so sure of mine and Morgan's rock-solid friendship, I'd almost be jealous of how well she and Berkley got along. If Morgan wasn't with me or at work, she was with him. Or we were all together. They were just as much best friends as she and I were, and I was happy about it, truly.

Berkley had become quite the staple in our lives. I asked constantly if there was something going on there, but she always made this disgusted face as if I'd accused her of being in love with her brother.

"We're definitely only friends. I haven't even thought of entertaining the idea," she'd said last time I asked her about it.

I'd have been lying if I said I didn't hope more would happen there. I wanted both of my good friends to be happy, but when I really paid attention to the way they were together and got serious brother-sister vibes, I dropped it for good.

"I'll have to see what I can get away with, but I'll try," I promised her.

"I'll go talk to Ms. Fisher myself if I have to. You're definitely coming with me. I don't want to sit there by myself all night," she whined.

"*Fine.* I'll do what I can and put the rest off for Monday."

She squealed and hugged me as we stepped up to the window to order our food.

After lunch I rushed through as many files as I could, leaving only three for Monday. I'd regret it, because it would mean staying extra late then, but I did want to go see Berkley play. Morgan and I went every chance we got to see his band, and we always had a lot of fun. I was drinking again, but not to excess this time around. I was still hurting, but I'd found better ways of coping rather than drinking myself into oblivion.

At five-thirty I was sweeping into the garage, my heels clacking against the concrete flooring, and I rushed to Morgan's car where she was waiting. A first. Typically, I was there before her.

"Let's go, let's go, we have to go get dressed," she chirped.

Back at my place, she dressed in a skintight black dress that fell above her knees and red heels that she'd brought along from home while we searched my closet for something for me to wear. Morgan pulled out a sleeveless lace red dress that made my boobs look awesome, but it didn't leave much to the imagination.

"What's the occasion? We're just going to see Berkley's band, right?"

"Yes, but I feel like dressing up tonight and I'm not doing it alone. I'll look stupid," she explained.

"Fine, but only this once." I changed into the dress, muttering my annoyance. It had a slit up the leg, right to the top of my hip. I'd worn it once to a work function and regretted it. I'd felt exposed all night, though I had to admit it did make me feel pretty sexy and confident. Two things I'd been lacking as of late.

Morgan did my makeup and hair after doing her own, and we rushed out the door. We were going to get there after they'd already gone on stage, but I didn't think it was really a big deal. Morgan, however, drove like the Devil was on her heels.

"What's the rush? We'll still get there in time to see the

rest of their set."

"I just don't want to miss anything is all."

I rolled my eyes and settled into the seat.

When we got there, we paid the door fee and entered, Morgan dragging me by my hand. Sure enough, we caught sight of Berkley's band on stage, Berkley banging his drumsticks against his drums in that wild, chaotic way he did when he was really into the music. I enjoyed watching him. To be so zealous over anything like that in life must be nice.

"Excuse us," Morgan yelled over the music while we pushed our way to the center of the crowd, which was odd since we normally hung back. I had no desire to be in the nosebleeds where people got rowdy.

Berkley looked up, scanning the crowd, and Morgan threw her hand up, jumping up and down to get his attention. When he saw us, he smiled and winked. Morgan and I danced along to the music, swaying our hips and laughing together. I was suddenly glad I'd come tonight instead of hanging around work. I always felt better after coming to one of Berkley's concerts, and tonight was no different.

When the song ended, I fanned my face with my hand and lifted my curly hair off my neck.

The lead singer of the band stepped up to the microphone. "Tonight, we have a little something special for you. This is for all you hopeless romantics out there."

The lights on the stage darkened and lit back up again momentarily. The lead singer was no longer in front of the microphone, but instead what I saw had my mouth dropping to the floor.

Hayden stood there, scanning the crowd until he spotted me. When his eyes met mine they sparkled, and his dimples deepened. The entire room was silent as he started speaking.

"I'm an idiot, in case none of you know me." Chuckles went up around the room. "You see, I love this girl more than anything, and I fucked it all up. And when I say I fucked it up, I mean I *fucked it up.* I hurt her very deeply, and that made me hurt. My whole life I never thought I was capable of loving someone the way I love her. Never have I felt so strongly for someone as I feel for her. She came into my life like a shooting star. Brilliant, but gone far too quickly. I almost lost her once before and I realized then how short life was. So I told her how I felt about her, and I never regretted it a second since. I had to go back to London to square some things away, and I've been gone exactly thirty-two days. Thirty-two days agonizing over whether or not she still loved me and wondering how in the hell I was going to fix the mess I made. I've had plenty of time to think about it, and I came to only one conclusion. I decided I was going to stand up here tonight and tell her in person that I've missed her a fuck of a lot and that I'll spend the rest of my life making up for what I've done, if that's what it takes."

He hopped down off the stage with the microphone, and the crowd parted when he moved forward. The spotlight followed him as he approached me. I glanced around, but even Morgan had moved back, so I was standing there alone in the middle of the crowd. I settled my gaze back on Hayden, who was now standing in front of me.

"I'm scared, fucking terrified of what I'm about to do, but I don't see any other way. Because for me, it's her or it's no one," he said, repeating his words from that last night I'd seen him all those days ago.

My heart raced, and he passed the microphone off to an audience member, digging into his pocket. He knelt in front of me on one knee and took my hand. My eyes widened, running over with tears.

"Juliet Banks, I love you. So much I can think of nothing but you every second of the day. I think of you before bed, I see you in my dreams, you're the first thing I think about when I wake up, and thoughts of you carry me through my day. You've consumed me completely." He opened the little box in his hands, staring down into it before turning his eyes back to me and holding the box up for me to see. "Make me happy tonight, and I promise you I will spend every day of our lives together making you just as happy. There won't be a day that goes by where I won't tell you how much I love you. I'll cherish you until I take my last breath, and that's a promise I intend to keep." He swallowed hard then said, "Marry me?"

I pressed my hand to my mouth to muffle my sob, sinking to the floor in front of him. Throwing my arms around his neck, I breathed him in. He still smelled minty and fresh just like he always had. Breaking away, I kissed him hard with trembling lips. My whole body was shaking, barely containing the emotions soaring through me.

"Yes," I whispered in his ear, and when I pulled back he was smiling widely.

He took the ring from the box and slid it into my finger, lacing his fingers through mine. Cheers and applause roared through the crowd around us, but I was deaf to it. In this moment, there was only Hayden and me.

I kissed him again, pressing my body into his, and his arms wrapped around me tightly. When the crowd settled down, Hayden stood and helped me off the floor into his chest. He smiled down at me with so much love it took the breath from my lungs. My face ached from the smile I couldn't seem to drop.

"Man am I glad you two got here on time," Berkley said to Morgan, throwing his arm around her shoulder.

I narrowed my eyes between them.

"You knew about this?" I asked her.

"Of course I did. Why did you think I was rushing to get here so fast? I love Berkley, but I've never once felt the need to break about fifteen laws just to get here in time to watch his band play."

He scowled at her and pinched her side. She elbowed him in the ribs.

I glanced between my friends and Hayden, realizing this had been planned for a while. How Morgan had managed to keep it from me was a miracle in itself. The girl couldn't keep her mouth shut about anything for very long. But between the man I loved and my two friends, I felt so much warmth radiating out from my chest, blooming and blossoming into the most beautiful feeling I'd ever experienced.

Hayden leaned down to talk into my ear. "Let's get out of here."

I turned to Morgan, who shooed me away. "Go, leave, you crazy kids. I'll hitch a ride with Berkley after the show."

I didn't stick around to ask her if she was sure. Hayden took my hand and led me toward the exit. People we didn't know stopped us to congratulate us on our way out the doors, and I thanked them quickly. Hayden didn't stop dragging me along, so I couldn't really stop to thank them properly.

He pressed me against the jeep and kissed me deeply, then hauled me up into the passenger seat, and we sped away toward my apartment.

We were barely in the door before he was on me, yanking the thin straps of my dress over my arms until it pooled at my feet. His mouth sucked at my collarbone, my neck, my chest. He was everywhere all at once.

Picking me up so I could wrap my legs around his waist, he carried me directly to bed and laid me on it with reverence. Peeling my panties down my legs, he stood over me, and when he began removing his shirt, I stopped him.

"Let me," I purred and roamed my hands over his warm skin, lifting his shirt over his head. I peppered kisses all over his chest and torso while working my hands at the button and zipper of his pants. I shoved them and his boxers off, and he stepped from them, gently pushing me onto the bed once more.

Capturing my mouth with his, he sank two fingers inside me and groaned. "Always so wet for me, aren't you, love?"

"Always," I breathed.

"This is going to be fast and hard, but I promise you, once I've gotten missing you out of my system, I'm going to take my time with you."

I shivered under that promise, and he aligned himself and sank into me on a powerful thrust.

Hours later we were a tangled mess of limbs lying in the middle of my bed, trying to catch our breath. True to his promise, he'd made love to me so tenderly over and over again after that first rough meeting. He was already making good on his oath to make me feel cherished and loved.

He rolled onto his side and propped his head up in his hand, peering down at me. A slow, sexy smile covered his face.

"What?"

"Juliet Noble. Has a nice ring to it, don't you think?"

My belly quivered, and I reached up to stroke his face. I answered his question with the touch of my lips to his.

"Are you happy, love?"

I didn't even have to think it over. "The happiest I've ever been."

"Good. You'll tell me if you ever aren't happy, right?"

"Like I'd be able to hide it from you if I wasn't."

He snorted and nodded.

"Fair enough." His gaze roamed my face while he continued to smile. "You're so beautiful, Juliet. And you're all mine. My future wife." He said it as if he could barely believe it were true.

"And you're all mine. My future husband."

He kissed my temple and dropped his head onto my shoulder.

"I love you more than anything," he whispered.

"I love you even more," I whispered back.

We lay quietly together for a long time before his soft, even breaths told me Hayden had fallen asleep. I wrapped my arm around him and held him close to me, afraid to go to sleep. Afraid this would all have been a dream and I'd wake up alone. But I knew this was real, it had to be. I gazed at my ring, a princess-cut glittering diamond nestled perfectly on my finger, and I knew that everything I ever wanted was going to come true for me for the first time in my life.

I wanted marriage and I wanted babies. I always had wanted to make a family of my own since having mine taken from me at such a young age. Once upon a time I had thought I'd have that with Drake someday, but I wouldn't trade what I had now for anything. Drake was like a distant memory that made me smile in remembrance. I'd never forget him as long as I lived, but more than anything, I thanked him. If it weren't for him, I would never have met Hayden. I would never have met this maddening, fiery, passionate man who made my blood pulse and sing.

"Thank you, Drake," I whispered into the air as I threaded my fingers through Hayden's dark locks.

I was in love — so in love it drove me mad. I'd been heartbroken and downtrodden by what had happened between Hayden and I, but in that month apart, my anger had waned to nothing more than a dying ember in a fire long since gone out. All I'd been left with then was that harrowing loneliness that came with missing him and the knowledge that I'd never loved anyone the way I loved him.

Berkley said he'd known early on that Hayden was a goner, when we'd gone bowling that night, but I think it was me who had been doomed from the start. From the moment Hayden had sat next to me in that bar, my fate had been sealed. And what a wonderful fate it was.

I sighed and studied Hayden's face. His long, dark lashes swept his cheeks, his full lips slightly parted. He was a beautiful man, and I had his love. Nothing in this world could feel better than that. I thought of every happy moment I'd had in life, and none compared to seeing him drop to his knee in front of me and ask me to marry him in a crowd full of strangers. I'd never forget tonight.

If knowing Hayden had taught me anything along the way, it was that I was capable of loving again, even more strongly than before. It had taught me that you can find what you're missing without even looking for it. And it had taught me to trust myself enough to take the risk. I'd taken a risk on Hayden, and it had been the best thing I'd ever done, because when I'd made that leap, he'd been right there at the bottom, waiting to catch me. And he'd continue to catch me every day for the rest of our lives.

Randy. He'd always been there for me. In fact, I couldn't even remember a time when he wasn't. But Bill Cambridge employed so many men, it was hard to keep track of them all. And given that my father's business practices were questionable at best, employee turnover was great. Around here, you learned not to get attached to people. Chances were they wouldn't be here long. My dad was not an easy man to get along with. Some guys chose to leave because they could not abide the man—others weren't as lucky.

I think the first time I really noticed Randy, I was about nine. I'd begun to wonder why my friends at school didn't have bodyguards around them all the time. Until then, I'd never really given it much thought. I assumed everyone lived the way I did. So, I began watching and listening to my surroundings.

It was then I noticed that everyone else was doing the same. All of my father's men were watchful. They not only kept tabs on my dad, but they were extremely vigilant when it came to visitors. And even more telling, my father's men watched each other. I thought they were all friends up until that day, until I realized not one of them trusted the others. You could see it on their faces. Man to man, they were cordial to one another, but as soon as one turned his back, a cloud of suspicion descended, marring the other's features.

I remember sitting on the edge of the in-ground pool watching and listening. I had decided to learn as many of their names as I could, and maybe even what specific position they held with my dad. I wasn't even exactly sure what it was my father did, but I was pretty sure it wasn't nice. I was bored and alone as usual and it seemed like a good game. April, my older sister by five years, was out. Not that she would have given me the time of day even if she'd been at home. She didn't like me much, but then again, she didn't seem to like many people.

That one, in the ill-fitting, grey pinstriped suit, his name was Buddy. I knew him. As much as Dad tried to keep us separate from them, there were still a few who were permanent fixtures and had been as far back as I could remember. Buddy was one of them. He was almost always at my father's side. His Right-hand man, I guessed.

Then there was Tom. He was just a very big man, tall and wide. I'd seen him shoulder more men than I could count out of my father's path. He would be his enforcer, I supplied.

Then there was Patrick. He was my favourite. He always had a piece of candy for me. But better than that, he was nice to me. He'd bandaged several skinned knees and he always seemed to know when I'd had a bad day at school. And on occasion, I sometimes even got a hug. My father and my sister were not huggers. At times it was nice to have someone hold you tight. It made me feel safe.

That day, I heard other names. Teddy, Jason, Gunner, Phil . . . And as I surveyed the yard, my gaze collided with another set of observant eyes.

His head was bent slightly forwards and his sandy-coloured hair covered his forehead. He looked as if he was ready to pounce right off the bar stool he was perched on. He seemed considerably younger than the rest of my father's associates, but much older than me, probably even older than my sister. He was wearing a worn white t-shirt and jeans, a brown leather cuff around his wrist. Not the usual uniform for their crowd either. I looked away quickly, but not before I saw his mouth quirk up in a grin.

Out of the corner of my eye, I saw him jump from the stool, coming my way. When he reached my position he rolled up the legs of his jeans, sat down beside me and dangled his feet into the warm water.

"Whatch'ya lookin' for, little one?" he asked.

"Nothing," I replied quietly, afraid I'd been caught doing something I shouldn't. I kept my head turned away from him.

"My name's Randy," he said. "You're Holly, right?"

He sounded like a nice boy. I turned to look at him. He was smiling at me. Now that I looked at him up close, he was older. He had stubble on his chin. His grey eyes twinkled as he watched me assessing him.

"How old are you?" I blurted before I could stop myself.

"I'm eighteen. How old are you?"

"Nine," I said, softly again and looked away. Eighteen! Wow! He was practically a man, I remembered thinking.

"Nine. Wow. You're really getting up there, aren't you?" he asked, sounding serious, though his voice made me think he might be smiling.

"I'll be ten in December," I said, trying to make myself sound older then wondering why I'd felt the need.

"Ah, yes, ten, I remember it well," he said, and something in his voice had changed. I looked back at him to see. The grin remained but no longer reached his eyes.

For some reason my usual shyness left me and I asked, "Did something happen to you when you were ten?" I observed him closely, trying to discover what made this seemingly happy boy-man sad.

"You are perceptive, aren't you, little one," he responded, but didn't answer the question.

"Why do you call me that?" Again, shyness, where art thou?

His expression turned severe and he raked his hand through his hair, making it curl and stand up on top. "Oops," he said, under his breath but I still heard him.

"I just wondered," I rushed, not liking that I'd made his smile vanish. "I've heard the other men say little one before. I just wondered at it. Never mind." I tried to make it better.

He looked down at my little hand patting his forearm just above the leather cuff.

I pulled my hand back quickly, mortified that I'd touched him.

To my surprise, he took my hand and placed it back on his arm. He took a deep breath and looked out over the pool. He nodded, as if he'd made a decision.

"Well, you know, all these men are here to ... uh," he pursed his lips for a moment, measuring his words, " ... help your father look after you and your sister, right?"

"Mmmhmm," I replied, awed that he was actually going to answer me. No one ever answered my questions.

"Well, we men," he puffed his chest out a bit too proudly, including himself with the elder group. "We have nicknames for you and your sister, so that other people won't know we're referring to you. And your dad doesn't like us to use your real names in public." He tapped my hand reassuringly. "Its just precaution. We're all just trying to keep you safe."

"Oh, like code. So, you call me little one."

"Yep, sometimes we just call you L.O."

"So, if I'm L.O., what do you call my sister?"

Ducking his head, he then smiled broadly. "We call her big one." I could tell he was trying not to laugh and I tried really hard to get the joke.

It wasn't until I said it out loud that I caught on. "That would make her B.O."

Unable to contain his amusement any longer he laughed out loud, a deep affecting sound that made me happy.

"She would have an absolute fit, if she knew that. Not only that you all call her big but that she stinks too." I giggled until my tummy hurt.

As we sat on the edge of the pool laughing together, Patrick approached us from the opposite side of the water. He didn't look happy like he usually did. Ever so slightly he raised his chin at Randy.

Randy scrambled to his feet and rolled down his jeans. As he bent on one knee he said under his breath, his lips barely moved. "I only told you that because you're almost ten and I know you are old enough to keep our secrets." With his sudden scrutiny, I knew he was asking me not to repeat what he'd confided in me.

"I won't tell, Randy," I said, seriously.

His features lightened and he smiled again. "I knew I could trust you, L.O."

He said it so fast as he started to get up I whispered, "That sounded like Lee Lo."

"Lee Lo," he smiled. "I like that." Then he hurried around to the other side of the pool where Patrick stood waiting for him.

Paddy said something to Randy that made him bow his head. His shoulders slumped.

I watched them walk away and I hoped I hadn't gotten Randy into trouble.

It wasn't until I couldn't see them anymore that I realized he'd never answered my question. What had happened to him when he was ten?

About the Author

Candace Ripley is a mother and girlfriend living in the mountains of North Carolina. In her spare time she likes to read anything she can get her hands on, knitting, and drinking tea.